HOTFOOT!

Tom Richards

POOKA
BASEMENT PRESS
Dublin

Copyright (c) Tom Richards 1995

DEDICATION

To Kristin, Cathy & Jonathan - my personal Hotfeet - and to Peter Thew - Guardian Angel First Class - whose advice helped make my wishes come true ...

First published in Ireland in 1995 by
Basement Press
an imprint of Attic Press
29 Upper Mount Street
Dublin 2

ISBN 1 85594 157 0

The moral right of Tom Richards to be identified as the Author of this Work is asserted.

Basement Press would like to thank CPC Foods Ltd, Ireland, for their support in the publication of this book.

Cover design: Dante Briscoe
Cover illustration: Jon Donoghue
Origination: Attic Press
Printing: The Guernsey Press Co. Ltd

This book is published with the assistance of The Arts Council/ An Chomhairle Ealaíon.

Chapter One

Earth has over five billion people bouncing around like lemmings all over its surface. Five billion of them! All of them wanting things. All of them hoping, wishing, praying - even stealing! (and we heartily disapprove of that, by the way) - for all of the stuff that they dream about.

Of those five billion souls, almost one thousand, two hundred and fifty million of them are thirteen years old and younger. These people wish for things too, of course. And in my job, that's a lot of wishes. And the things that they wish for! Bikes top the list. Followed by CD players, concert tickets, televisions, and ghetto blasters. All of these wishes get shot into space - great blue bolts of wishes zooming way up beyond the stratosphere. Once they get up here, a gang of angels - new recruits, you know, just out of their skins and serving their apprenticeship - they catch all these wishes in giant wish containers, sort them into different categories by age, sex and variety, and hand them over to the senior staff who organise this rainbow of dreams into some kind of recognisable list.

The worst time is Christmas. We get absolutely snowed up here at Christmas time; you wouldn't believe the avalanche of wishes that we get. But that's another story, and I'd better stick with the one

I came here to tell.

Now, about wishes ... most of the time, we do what we can. Senior staff will have a word in the appropriate ear. Usually a parent or a grandparent. An aunt, uncle - even a teacher, if we think they might do anything about it. Senior staff sort of put a thought here. A niggling suggestion there. And it usually works out. As I say, that's their job. And when they can make a dream come true - well, it's sort of satisfying, isn't it?

But then, there are those other wishes. Those ones that are almost impossible to make come true. When they come blowing up here out of the stratosphere, the apprentices aren't really sure what to do with them. They get categorised into Problem Wishes - and then they pass them on to me. Because that's what I do. I work on problem wishes, and try to sort things out. A problem wish may be something simple: for instance, a boy really wants a dog and the parents hate dogs. Or a girl might want to be transformed into a pop star - someone like Madonna, for instance. Of course, there already is a Madonna - so that's kind of impossible to make come true. Know what I mean?

But the all-time impossible wishes are from the kids who want to become professional football players. You wouldn't believe how many kids want to spend an entire lifetime kicking a little white ball around a grass-covered field. To me, it sounds a little crazy. I mean, what kind of proper job is that?

Despite my own opinions, I do what I can of course. And every now and then I get lucky, and a kid goes on to become a megastar with Liverpool or

Chelsea or - what's that other one? - oh, yes. Of course. Manchester United. But you just wouldn't believe how many young people want to become football heroes! And now, even some of the girls have this at the top of their all-time wish list. And football clubs aren't even signing girls.

Needless to say, I can't help everyone. There just aren't enough places to fill all the wishes. And if I get a football wish from someone who just can't play - well, what's an angel to do, for Gosh sakes?

Unfortunately, there are other ways to have your wishes granted. Bad and evil ways. Ways which I don't even want to talk about, really. A couple of people you might have heard about tried making their wishes come true this way, and it didn't work. People like Adolf Hitler and Jesse James and that Roman emperor, Nero. That's a few of them. They didn't get an answer quick enough, I guess. Wouldn't use the usual channels and wait for their wishes to come true like everyone else. Instead, they got a little visit from a fellow I know. Rather a rough chap, I think, called Lucky Lucy. He talked to the people I just mentioned. Told them a bunch of lies. Also told them that their wishes would be granted darned quick if they'd sign his little bitty piece of paper. Of course, they never read the fine print. So, they decided to take up his offer - and I shudder to think about the consequences.

But I warned them. I warned them all! But did they listen when I warned them about Lucky? Nope. 'Drop dead,' they said to me. Went off and did things their way - and look where it got them. And the fact that they'll spend the rest of eternity in a permanent Turkish steam bath somewhere below ground isn't any of my business, either. They made their choice, and now they have to take the consequences.

Most of the time, anyway. But every now and then, a special case comes along. One where the person was just too young - or too stupid - to know better. In those instances, I try to turn things around. Get the contract with Lucky broken. Make certain that the poor kids don't spend the rest of Time shovelling coal.

Which brings me to my story. See, there was this kid. And boy oh boy, did he want to play football. He drooled all over the place when he even thought about the game. Of course, I did everything I could do to help. But he just didn't have the knack to play, know what I mean? Then, along comes Lucky Lucy. I tried to warn the kid. I tried! And he almost lost everything. But you'll find that out later.

For now, the story starts with a day-dream ...

' ... and we have one minute, thirty seconds remaining in injury time! Manchester United one; Arsenal one. This is it! With only seconds left, Man United desperately need another score to ensure their advance toward the Premier League Championship.'

The Man United rookie, brought in only a month ago, listened to the match on the old portable radio hanging in the player's dugout. He could hear the announcer breathe deeply, catching his breath, trying his best not to gag on the flapping, professional tongue. The rookie shifted his head abruptly, looking back out on to the field. The teams were moving like silk across the green carpet of the pitch.

Above them, surrounding the two teams, one hundred thousand fans shouted, pleading for a score, their huge combined voice rolling across the field, hitting him almost physically.

We have to win this! he thought. As if in answer to his prayers, he saw the striker disengage from a pack, winning the ball. The striker - his famous team-mate - ran quickly, surely down the pitch, eyes on the net, making certain of his strike. Then, from behind him, a blur of the defender rushed toward him. The striker tripped, staggering. Then the two tumbled, striking the ground hard. And the Manchester United player stayed on the wet pitch, unmoving.

The radio announcer's voice stopped suddenly, seeming to hang in mid-air for a moment. 'What's this? What's this? Oh, what a blow for Manchester United! Cole has fallen! The trainer is running across the pitch! The brilliant Manchester United striker is being taken off the field. And that must surely be it for the great Man United striker. And the crowd is going wild! Surely, Arsenal will get the draw. And that will be the end of the great Manchester dream,' the announcer continued, his voice tight and drawn.

'The question now: who will be thrown into this match at such a critical moment? Who will the Manchester United manager call upon on such a momentous occasion?'

The rookie was on his feet, staring out across the field. Yes! It was true! Cole had been injured. They'd have to field another striker, and be quick about it. But who? His eyes wormed their way down the line of substitute players, looking for the man who would make that important decision. The rookie dared to hope that he would be put into the match. But how could he? That dream was impossible! The young rookie could only stand by the line and wait like everyone else.

Then he saw the manager point with that strong, certain forefinger down the line of players. Pointing - towards him. *Was it possible? The manager was waving his arm at him now, beckoning.* Yes! thought the rookie. *Yes! It's me!*

And the radio announcer roared, 'It's the rookie! Manchester United are placing their hopes in the raw new recruit! A recruit with so much untested, yet certain talent! What a tremendous decision! What a moment!'

The rookie ran out across the pitch between the line of opposing players, trading verbal jabs. He took up his position. *Keep it easy. Head up. Eyes on the ball way down at the other end of the field.* His eyes roved quickly to his team captain. He saw the brief hand-signal. Felt the eyes of the midfielders on him. He took in a ragged breath of air, letting it out uneasily between a clenched jaw. His eyes flashed for a moment to the referee. *Only forty seconds,* he guessed. *Only forty seconds until the end of the match. And in that time we have to score.*

The Man United keeper booted the ball. He watched as it floated, fifteen or twenty metres up. *Floated forever. Coming down, now. Down to hit the midfielder on the chest, controlling it.* The rookie moved forward, running now, beating the defensive player. *Can't be off-side,* he thought, slowing up for a moment, then looking behind him.

The ball was coming upfield fast, dribbling between the magic feet of his team-mate. The tremendous forward roamed toward the rookie for a moment, then split suddenly cross field. A group of defenders fell toward the

8

ball, *trying to stop the Man United player's forward momentum.*

The rookie caught an Arsenal defender careening toward him. He faked easily, stepping forward, feinting to the left, upfield. The defender followed. The rookie's feet stopped, shifted direction, moving into midfield. The defender, faked out, was behind him now.

The ball was fifteen metres from him. Three defenders were on it; the Manchester player feinted right, left, right - stroking the ball magically between his running feet, drawing the defenders in. Suddenly, he turned on the speed, running two metres forward, kicking it deftly with his left foot, the ball drifting up past their heads, almost in slow motion. Reaching its zenith, the ball dropped toward him. The rookie striker stood, ready, the defender guarding him trying to recover his position; running up toward him now. He could see the fear in the player's eyes. And the fear told him that he had won.

The ball floated out of space toward the rookie. He was ready. He would not let the ball touch the ground. Not this time. He would do it all at once, neatly and gracefully. The ball was at head height; falling, floating. He stepped forward on to his right foot. The ball was there. His senses told him where the net was. Just there, he thought. The keeper just there, out of position.

His left leg moved forward. Bone and flesh and boot met the ball solidly. WHACK! He heard it. Felt it. The sound of a solid strike. Picking his head up, he watched it. Watched as it rocketed - R O C K E T E D - past the dumbfounded defence, past the outstretched arm of the desperate Arsenal keeper. Watched it all the way in as it hit the back of the net, rocking it, swinging wildly, the keeper splayed helplessly on the ground in front of the

9

goalposts like a defeated warrior.

And then he heard the crowd roar his name, and he could almost see it soaring into the four corners of Old Trafford stadium, and into football history: 'LARKIN! LARKIN! LARKIN! LARKIN!'

'Larkin. Hey, Larkin! Get over here!' Gerry Larkin sat on the sodden grass in his old yellow and purple tracksuit bottoms, the dream shattering at the sound of his name. He unwound his long body and stood up, wiping a few blades of mouldy turf from his wet bottom.

Joe McNamara pointed to him accusingly, the permanent frown covering his red face. 'What's wrong with you? Can't you hear, either? Jeez, you're stupid, Larkin.'

Gerry Larkin didn't say a word. Instead, he walked over to join the other six lads on the team. Every night it was the same old stuff, he thought. He'd rush out after school, grab a Twix at McKeever's shop, and walk to the small field where he'd try to get into the game. The same fourteen lads would always show up. The Barkley brothers - Clay and Gunner - George Smith, Alan Wilder, Richard Markey and the rest. And always they would have the same two team captains: Joe McNamara and Larry O'Shay. Except for Gerry Larkin, the two were the biggest of the lot and the best players. It was only natural that they would assume leadership.

And that they would pick teams.

Gerry Larkin hated that part. He was the worst player. The very worst. Gerry Larkin didn't mind much, at least he thought he didn't mind. He couldn't help it if he wasn't super-coordinated. There were more important things in life, weren't there? Well, maybe ...

In the group of lads that showed up every night, he was certainly the worst player. And because of this he was always chosen last. Last. Like the hard burned bits that no one wants at the bottom of a bag of popcorn. And Gerry Larkin knew that he was lucky to be chosen at all.

His team-mates grumbled, annoyed that they had to play with the loser. 'Hey, McNamara. Do we have to let him play? Remember last time?' Wilder said. Wilder was the shortest member of the team, a head shorter than Gerry Larkin. Still, he was valued by the rest.

The team laughed, their voices drilling a hole in Gerry's soul. He remembered the last time he had played, of course. Only yesterday. Remembered when the ball had finally come bouncing toward him. He had run toward it, sure of himself. Making certain that this time ... this time ... it would be right! He'd feed the ball in, past that grinning Gunner Barkley, drilling it right past his nose and into the gaping net. It hadn't worked out that way, of course.

He had stopped. Placing his right foot firmly on the wet grass, he felt himself slipping. His lousy cleats couldn't gain a proper hold on the slick surface. It wasn't right, he knew, but he was committed. He looked up. Barkley was running toward him, shouting, waving his stupid arms, trying to block him. He had to strike now, or

Barkley would be all over him. He swung his left leg with all the power that he could muster, feeling the foot reach out, reaching into space to drill it into the target ... and watched as his foot missed the ball - watched as Barkley's savage face left his field of vision ... seeing now the grey clouds as the momentum from his gigantic strike took him completely off his feet. Falling. Crashing flat on his back.

And the howls of laughter drifted in from the field, from the twisted mouths of his so-called friends.

That had been yesterday. Today, they were arguing about who would get stuck with the Loser Larkin yet again. And Gerry Larkin could only hope that they would let him play ...

McNamara stepped forward a little, confronting Alan Wilder. 'We gotta let him play,' McNamara stated sourly. 'If he doesn't play, we're one man short. And that means *you* don't play. Get it, Wilder?' The short lad nodded grimly, like a guy who knew that he had to eat broccoli even though he hated the stuff.

'OK,' the captain stated, certain that he had put a stop to this breach of his authority. 'Let's beat these guys. Come on!' The rest of the team took the field. But McNamara stopped Gerry Larkin from running out on to the pitch with a large hand placed squarely on his heaving chest. 'Did you hear that, Larkin? We're going to beat these guys today. So don't mess up. Otherwise ...' His red face glared into Larkin's, and the other hand rolled itself into a fist, cocking itself just under Gerry's nose. 'You.

Will. Never. Play. Here. Again. Got it?'

Gerry Larkin nodded slowly. 'I understand. Don't mess up. I won't,' he replied weakly. McNamara studied him sharply, the small ugly eyes glowering under their thick eyebrows. Then he ran out and joined the rest of the team, Gerry Larkin following in his wake.

Looking back on this last match with the McNamara team, Gerry Larkin could only think that it was one of the worst moments of his life. Which only made the rest of his life seem that much worse ...

Gerry Larkin was eleven years old, and constantly teased about the fact that he was the son of the local police sergeant. Gerry had no ambition to follow in his father's footsteps, however. For Larkin, there was only one ambition. Gerry Larkin wanted to play soccer. Professional soccer. He lived the game. Breathed it. Prayed about it. His room was plastered with posters of his favourite players. He followed all of the teams religiously. During the 1994 World Cup, Gerry Larkin had to be banished from the living room every night at midnight - otherwise, his parents knew, he would have stayed up until dawn every morning, watching the highlights on the ancient telly.

And while many of his other classmates dreamed of becoming doctors, solicitors, engineers, pilots - even Indian chiefs - Gerry Larkin knew in his heart that for him there was only one option - football.

But Gerry Larkin knew that he had a major problem. It was simple. Gerry Larkin couldn't play.

Try as he might, he couldn't get the hang of handling the stupid, round, innocent-looking ball.

Part of the problem lay in Gerry's height. At the ripe old age of eleven, Larkin was already five foot eight inches tall. His mother said that he was all arms and legs. Then she'd always laugh a little, trying to make him feel better. 'Ah, but give it a couple of years, Gerard!' (She always called him 'Gerard' when they were at home, and he hated it.) 'When you're grown, you'll be a fine-looking giant of a young man! Then, everyone will want you on their football team!'

Great, he thought. I'm going to be a giant. A complete freak. And it's only going to take a couple of years for this strange event to reach finality.

Looking in the full-length mirror behind his mother's wardrobe, he pondered on the monstrous size of his body. His arms hung down from a weak chest like some sort of degenerate ape's. His legs were long and stringy, shaped like two lengths of rubber garden hose. Of even more frustration, however, was the fact that these horrendous appendages simply refused to obey him. No matter what his brain might order, each of his arms and legs had a mind of its own.

Pretty difficult, he considered sullenly, having a body with five brains. One brain in each arm. A brain in each leg. And a command centre in his own brain desperately fighting for control.

This meant that those very same arms and legs constantly disobeyed him. They formed a tangled spider's web of obnoxious flesh and bone, always managing to move themselves into complicated

14

positions from which there was no escape.

He remembered vividly the time when he had tripped coming through the family kitchen, bumping into his mother, her outstretched hands attempting to steady the pile of dirty dinner dishes which she had just taken up from the table. He watched horrified as the plates tipped unsteadily. That decisive command centre of his quickly put through the orders to the arms. Unfortunately, they chose their own course. He watched, feeling as if he was in a dream, as his traitor arm reached up to help her, pushing rather than pulling. And he could only watch stupidly as the plates fell into the pile of clean glasses, newly purchased from the shop ... CRASHING ... then careening on toward the standing porcelain china, the forty-year-old valuable china which his grandmother had cherished ... the whole pile, dirty dishes, cold mashed potatoes from the dinner, leftover carrots, glinting glasses, white china - plunging to the tiled floor. And there - SHATTERING. Porcelain-potato-china-carrot-dishes - a mess of mucked-up stuff that was now junk. And he was responsible. Yet again.

His mother could only look at him.

It was the same in football.

Yet it was not his worst moment. No. Looking back, he knew that the very worst moment of his life had been this one final match for the McNamara team - this one final, horrible, stupendously idiotic match when he knew that life was no longer worth living.

With McNamara's threat still ringing in his ears, Gerry Larkin had taken the field. 'I will *not* mess up!' he repeated to himself over and over. He ordered it to the clopping legs as they moved over the slick green of the rough pitch. 'I will *not* mess up!' he commanded the dangling arms as they pumped aimlessly at his sides, the long thin fingers not quite certain how or where to tuck themselves into his palms.

Today, he was playing midfield - sort of. It could be midfield or back or centre or striker. With a small team it just depended on where the ball went, and the luck of the draw on the day. Gerry Larkin waited. Waited until the ball was in motion. And he started running.

Gerry Larkin ran like a giraffe. His huge feet attached to his skinny legs clopped along in an uncoordinated assault on the tufts of grass beneath them. His head stuck out on a long, skinny, rather fragile-looking barge-pole of a neck. It wobbled as he ran, and worse still, his Adam's apple visibly bobbed up and down - like a sort of yo-yo - as he breathed in and out.

But despite the rather inept look of a charging animal - which should rightly be found only in the local zoo - Gerry Larkin didn't care because he was playing football!

The first part of the match was fine. He made it without messing up for a full fifteen minutes. During that time, he had worked hard, running in his ungainly fashion to keep up with the ball, getting up a tremendous sweat. But for the most part, and despite his hard work, Gerry Larkin didn't do much during the first fifteen minutes of the match because his team-mates made certain that he didn't get the ball. Dribbling it first one way, then the other, always past him, always out beyond him to McNamara or Gunner or that nerd Wilder, they kept the ball away from him. But it didn't matter. No it didn't! he thought wildly. Because I'm playing!

Yet, even Gerry Larkin's patience had a limit. When he realised that his team-mates were not going to let him have the ball, he got embarrassed, then angry. Finally, he had enough. 'Hey, let me have a chance with the ball!' he shouted to McNamara. The team captain, playing keeper, and happy that he had managed to keep Larkin's involvement in the match down to a minimum, only leered.

'Naw, you're playing fine as you are. Besides, we're winning!'

True enough, thought Gerry. They were ahead, now, three-two. And for a minute, that in itself was satisfying.

The other side was growing despondent. He watched Alan and Rick O'Neill, defenders on the other team, pace back toward their own goal, hands in pockets, counting the time until they could call it quits. Only five more minutes left in the match. Five more minutes, then they'd all have to go home for dinner and homework. But the score was three-two. And that was all that mattered. If they could keep it that way, they'd win. And Gerry Larkin would have played his part in the win simply by being on the field.

Standing near his own goal, Gerry looked up. It was a line-out, he noticed. The other team had the ball. Larry O'Shay, the captain of the opposing team, stood at the line, running his hands roughly over his wet jersey. He looked out, surveying the lay of the land like a young hunter searching for the perfect shot. His arms moved up, hands cradling the ball, grasping it tightly, now. Throwing!

Larkin, suddenly determined to get into the match, moved uncertainly toward midfield, forcing his giant frame into a resemblance of a trot. The ball, painted for a moment in the colours of the setting sun, hit the ground with a smack just yards from him. The defence - his team! - swarmed through the opposition, trying to lay waste to the tiring offence. It was only time, Larkin knew, before his team would win control again. He glanced at his watch. Almost five, he thought. Only a couple of more minutes.

And then, Gerry Larkin did a dumb thing. He looked up. Right into the blinding sun. He stood there, mystified, staring at it as if he had never seen the sun before. And then, when he looked down, he discovered something remarkable. He couldn't see anything. Not clearly, anyway. There was this one big, ridiculous black spot in the middle of his vision, and everything else seemed to be in shadows, like a black and white TV gone crazy.

He looked up again. Maybe it wouldn't make any difference being blind, he thought. Besides, the action was way over there on the other side of the pitch. And they haven't let the ball come near me anyway.

And then, it happened. The ball skittered across the wet grass, landing right under him. At his feet.

He looked down, still half-blind, barely making out the circle of leather lying invitingly at his toes. His large head roved around, trying to find the other players. All he could see were these floating blobs zooming around on the other side of the pitch, like a bunch of madmen trying to play hide-and-seek at midnight.

Gerry Larkin shook his head, feeling the sweat break out suddenly on his brow. This is it! he thought. My moment. *'My moment!'* he screamed.

He turned the ball quickly, his large feet obeying his brain for a change. Moving the ball downfield, his vision started to clear, and he rubbed his eyes brutally as he ran, forcing them to work. He turned his head, searching again for the opposing players, the cruel defence that would surely try to deny him this one single drive toward a goal and personal glory. And as he ran, he realised that a miraculous thing was happening. The players - all of them - seemed to drift away from him, peeling back as if he were a charging bull or a runaway truck - or a superstar.

He ran and ran, hearing the cheers of his team as he charged toward a certain goal. In that moment, Gerry Larkin was all the people he had ever dreamed of. He was Pelé. Paul Gascoigne. Diego Maradona. He would prove what he was made of. He would show McNamara and all the others that he wouldn't mess up. The moment was his! And he would score!

Gerry Larkin dribbled astutely downfield, plodding along this time with new confidence. Now, he was just in front of the net. In his excitement, he never considered why the keeper should be so far out of position. He knew only that the goal was his for the taking.

Rearing back now with his long, long right leg, he felt the power there. Felt the power coiling into a loaded spring which would deliver this time for sure! And he shot, feeling the certainty of the strike, watching now as the ball moved gracefully up in a great arc. Watching as its neat whiteness buried itself in the back of the net.

He had scored, he realised suddenly. HE. HAD. SCORED!

Gerry Larkin heard the roars behind him turn to anguish. His vision was clear, now. And then he realised what he had done. And he thought he was going to puke.

Gerry Larkin had scored ... an OWN GOAL.

And as he realised the magnitude of the disaster, as he heard the roars of curses from his fellow team-mates, he ran as fast as he could away from the field, hearing only one phrase from McNamara ringing into his fiery-red ears: 'Never NEVER PLAY HERE AGAIN!'

Chapter Two

'So, whad'ya going to do about it?'

Gerry Larkin stood next to Fran Clifford. Fran Clifford was a year older than Gerry. She was also considerably shorter. At full height, she stood only as tall as Gerry's chest. But Larkin liked her. She was smart, determined, and - most importantly - Gerry Larkin's best friend.

They stood in his front drive, kicking an old football heavily against the garage door. He turned to her, gazing down on Fran from his fantastic height. 'Don't know,' he sighed. 'Guess I'll never play again.'

'Horse-manure,' she said. 'I thought you loved playing football.'

He nodded glumly, and felt tears welling up into his eyes. 'Yep. That's true. I dream about it. Pray about it. Last week I said a hundred Hail Marys. One hundred of them!' he said thickly, as if this would guarantee his entry into the football hall of fame. 'I just want to play football. That's all I want to do!'

'So,' Fran said somewhat snidely, 'do it.'

Gerry shook his head dismally. 'Nope. I can't.'

'What do you mean you can't,' she said darkly.

'I can't,' he said again.

'What?' Frances Bernadette Mary Therese said,

her voice screeching up an octave.

'I can't!' he replied, 'I'll never be able to play football again. And there's nothing I can do to change that.' And when he had finally closed his mouth on these perfectly sincere words, Gerry Larkin knew that he had made a grave mistake.

Because Fran couldn't stand the words 'I can't'. And when she heard those words, she got mad ... Frances Bernadette Mary Therese Clifford was always getting mad. She was from a family who always got mad. They got mad because they wouldn't put up with anything that they didn't like. And rather than like it, they'd get mad and set out to make things so that they did like it. It was as simple as that. And one thing was for certain. No Clifford had ever said, 'I can't.' The whole town knew that this was a trait that ran deep in the entire family. From tottering old Grandpa Clifford right down to three-year-old Runty Clifford, the words 'I can't' simply weren't in their vocabulary. Instead, they'd just get mad - and try to change the world.

Which is what Fran Clifford was now considering. When Frances Bernadette Mary Therese Clifford got angry, she would get real quiet. Sort of as if she was waiting for a train or for a kettle to boil. People who didn't know her would think that Fran Clifford was just getting depressed or dazed or something. She'd stand with her arms crossed, her long, jet-black hair hanging straight down, her brown eyes gazing out into space as if she'd gone stupid. Of course, people who knew her also knew that something else was going on behind those crazed-looking eyes.

And when Gerry Larkin, snivelling in his drive, looked up to find Fran Clifford gazing off into space, he knew that there was bound to be trouble. And, if things went as usual, the trouble would soon be his own. 'Uh-oh,' he whispered. Gerry Larkin scuffed the drive slowly with his old runners. He coughed. He flapped his long monkey arms around. He sat down suddenly on the ground and stood up again. He banged the football as hard as he could against the aluminium garage door. He created a racket. Gerry Larkin tried anything to get the wheels turning in Fran Clifford's head to grind to a halt. But there was no going back. He knew it.

The frozen gaze on Fran Clifford's face broke. A smile formed. The ends of her short lips raised themselves in a Cheshire Cat smile that even Alice herself would have been proud of.

Fran Clifford turned. She walked slowly over to where Gerry Larkin stood, scowling. He held his breath, waiting for the remark that he knew might change his world. What's she thinking of? he wondered. Murdering McNamara, maybe?

She stood right next to him, her head cocked back so that she could look directly up into her friend's somewhat frightened eyes. Fran Clifford cleared her throat. 'We're going to form our own team.'

'Form our own team?' he repeated stupidly.

'Sure. Why not?' she stated, matter-of-factly.

Gerry Larkin stood there, stunned. He hadn't thought of that! And why should he when he had Fran Clifford to do all the thinking for him?

Chapter Three

Gerry and Fran were on the school field, trying to put their team-recruitment strategy into some sort of order. Fran marched up and down the field in front of Gerry, beat a small, round hand into a tiny fist. 'This is going to be our team!' she cried.

'Right!' Gerry agreed.

'A team that will make a difference!' she yelled.

'Right again!' Gerry agreed.

'A team that will make history!' she shouted.

'Make history?' he said uncertainly. 'How's it going to make history? All I want to do is play football. I don't care too much about making history.' He sat down abruptly, not caring if he got his school trousers a little wet. Carefully, he crossed his long legs. 'So who are we going to get to play?'

Fran Clifford walked over to him. She was all fired up with the thoughts of a winning football team. A team that could take on the best that any other school would field.

For secretly Fran Clifford had always wanted to play football. She had always wanted to play keeper. And despite her size, Fran knew that she could be a great keeper. A fantastic keeper. As good, maybe, as Packie Bonner. All right, maybe not quite as good. But close, anyway ...

But Fran knew that she had two things against

her. First of all, she was a girl. And any team worth its salt wouldn't put up with a girl on its side. They'd consider committing suicide first. Second, she was short. Very short. She was the shortest person in her class; short legs, short arms. She was not exactly the stuff that great keepers were made of.

Yet, when she had formulated the fantastic idea of forming their own team, she thought that in one fell swoop she might change the world. And that included becoming a great keeper. Despite being a girl, and despite her rather short size.

And now, marching up and down past Gerry Larkin on the green grass of a football field, she thought that she might make her dream come true. In her mind, she could see the stunning national headlines: FRAN CLIFFORD SAVES INTER-NATIONAL MATCH, read one. STICKYFINGERS CLIFFORD PRIDE OF IRISH TEAM, read another.

It was possible. With a little luck, why not?

She turned to her friend. 'We'll get anyone who wants to play to play with us!' she shouted suddenly. 'This will be a team of dreamers! A team of people who have never been given a chance! You'll see, Gerry. This will be a team of giants!'

Gerry Larkin, glancing down at his long frame, could only agree.

And so it was that their team came into being. Fran and Gerry worked hard to form that team. And they did what they could to pick the best.

But they had a problem. They could only get those people who couldn't play with anyone else.

25

Like Gerry Larkin himself, these were the kids that didn't seem to matter. But Fran and Gerry knew that all that really mattered was that they played football.

'It doesn't matter who we choose,' Gerry stated. 'Just as long as we all get the chance to play.'

Frances nodded her head in agreement. 'Right you are!' she said positively. 'I don't care if we don't win one game. The whole point here is to play football!' She wagged a finger in front of Gerry's long nose. 'But you just wait. We're going to show McNamara. We'll practice. We'll work hard! We'll play smart!' Her determined eyes again saw headlines. 'We'll be the greatest, and we won't let anyone kick us around again!'

Gerry nodded his head uncertainly, wondering how they were going to pull off this miracle. But, despite Fran's dreams of greatness, they went to work and got a team together.

They got Tommy Reynolds to play with them. They decided that he would play in midfield. Reynolds wore glasses that were so thick that you could use them as a magnifying glass. Gerry Larkin had often used the heavy lenses to start small fires in the woods where he and Tommy would sit roasting ants or worms or anything else that had the bad fortune to come along.

Sitting in the woods, Gerry had noticed that Tommy couldn't see much without his glasses. When he talked with him about joining the team, Gerry asked what would happen if he lost his glasses during a match. 'Don't worry,' Tommy said cheerily. 'I won't lose them.' Gerry wasn't at all sure

about that, but decided to take Tomm... ...
it.

Big Jimmy agreed to play centre-fo... ...
Jimmy was called 'Big Jimmy' because h... ...
that - big. He had tried dieting, exercise - ...
mum had even had him hypnotised - but ...n no
luck. He just couldn't lose weight. When Big Jimmy
ran it was like watching a tonne and a half of loose
lard wash down the field. The only good thing was
the fact that no one cared to defend Big Jimmy.
Because if anyone got in Big Jimmy's way, he was
dead. Rolled over on impact. Flattened, squashed
and forgotten. It's a fact, and more than one person
has been fortunate enough to live to tell the tale.

Then there was Harold Smyth. Harold had a
problem. Harold was afraid of getting hit. By
anything. He didn't particularly like playing sports.
He abhorred rugby, hurling, Gaelic football - any
kind of contact sport. And he particularly detested
soccer.

And if he was hit - by a ball or a kid or a
bounding dog or a frisbee - Harold Smyth would
break out crying. He'd stand there in the field, and
the tears would well up out of his wishy-washy
green eyes, and he couldn't stop them.

By this time, Fran and Gerry were getting a little
desperate. They were having trouble getting
enough kids together to form a team, and so they
decided to bribe Harold Smyth into playing. 'We'll
give you a week's supply of crisps,' Fran started,
'and all you have to do is play football for us.'

Harold said he didn't know. 'Besides, those other
kids are big. You know?' he said in that cringing

_e of his.

Gerry took a long look at Fran, realising that they would have to up the ante if they were going to convince Harold to play. 'A week of crisps,' Gerry said smoothly, 'and I'll give you half of my bottle of squash at lunch for an entire month. Just don't get any grungy bits into it when you're taking a slug, and I won't mind. Honest.' Gerry didn't like squash too much anyway, so it wasn't a particularly difficult sacrifice.

Harold shook his head. 'It's not antiseptic,' he said. 'I could catch a disease from you and get sick or die or something.'

Fran was losing her patience. 'Then you can drink your half first, Harold!' she said threateningly.

Harold knew Fran well enough to know what would happen if he made her angry. That said, he wondered if he should push his luck a little. His small face considered his next move, the thin lips carefully forming a question. 'What about a bar?' he asked abruptly. 'Lunch isn't the same without a bar for dessert.'

Fran looked at him, and Harold knew that he'd pushed his luck too far. 'OK,' he said lamely, back-pedalling before he lost the crisps and the squash. 'No bar. When do we start playing?'

The deal was done, and Harold was told to play opposite Tommy Reynolds in midfield.

The team needed two more players, they knew. Two more players, and the team of their dreams would be reality at last! Fran and Gerry thought about it for a while, running through the kids that they had not yet approached. Most had said 'No!', of course, which left them with few options. They were running out of possible players, when Fran thought of the twins.

These were the Bright Brothers: Almost and Not Quite. That's honestly what they were called. They were both pretty stupid. Both of them were in sixth class, and neither of them could read too well. They tried hard, of course, but they just couldn't get the hang of it. The real problem seemed to be that they had trouble remembering things, like words and names and numbers and rules and orders and ... well, almost anything.

Fran talked to them about joining up. She knew how much they liked playing football. And McNamara wouldn't even be bothered with them. The twins, blinding red hair shaved short and faces covered with freckles, both thought for a moment, then nodded vigorously. Sort of like a pair of matching orange Erasure-heads, she thought absently, relieved when they both agreed to play defence.

She just hoped that they would remember to show up to the games.

The newly appointed players assembled for the first time in the football field on the Tuesday after school. Gerry Larkin looked them over: Almost and Not Quite Bright, Tommy Reynolds, Big Jimmy, Harold Smyth, Fran Clifford and himself. The seven of them.

Fran Clifford cleared her throat roughly, her small form marching surely down the line of lads. 'This is it. We're a team!' she said. 'And we're going to play football!'

'What are we going to call ourselves?' Big Jimmy said out of the corner of his pumpkin-sized face. He'd come along wearing a large grey sweatshirt, and he looked like a blimp getting ready to make a difficult landing.

Fran thought about it for a minute. 'Well,' she said, 'to be honest, the team was my idea. But I got the idea from Gerry. So,' she breathed in deeply, a smile growing on her dark face, beaming out at her team-mates. 'I propose that we call ourselves Larkin's Lot!'

They all cheered. Gerry Larkin looked at the six of them, kind of embarrassed. 'You sure you want to name the team after me?'

Fran turned on him. 'Well who else do you want to name it after, Snow White? I thought you'd be pleased, having the team named after you.'

He stood there, his head shaking uncertainly on the long pole that was his neck. 'I don't know. McNamara might laugh at it.'

'McNamara. McNamara!' she cried. 'Forget McNamara! The seven of us are going to play football! We're going to do what we've always wanted to do! Despite the McNamaras of this world.' The rest of the team erupted into a crazed banshee of noise. Only Larkin stood there unsmiling.

Fran Clifford interrupted the cheering. 'That's enough noise. We gotta save our strength. Because I got news. We're playing our first match tomorrow!'

'What do you mean, tomorrow?' Gerry said, speaking for all the rest of them. This first match was news to Gerry. He turned his lengthy frame toward the small friend, wondering, frightened. 'We can't play tomorrow. We haven't even had a practice. How can we possibly play anybody when we haven't even had a chance to practise?' His Adam's apple bobbed visibly beneath his pointed chin. 'And,' he sniffed, 'You could at least let us know who we're playing.'

'Cheer up, Gerry. You look like your dog just died and was eaten by cannibals. Of course we can play tomorrow. We're Larkin's Lot and we can play anybody, any time!' Fran almost sang this announcement in excitement. The team copied her with much less enthusiasm, the voices dying like a drowned cat's.

'As for who we're playing. That's the best surprise of all!' She gazed at the others as if she was letting them in on the biggest secret of all time.

'McNamara,' she said wickedly. 'We're going to play McNamara!'

And Gerry Larkin wanted to die and forget the whole thing.

31

Chapter Four

Looking back on it, I can't help but understand why the kids did what they did. In my capacity as Problem Wish Assistant First Class, and gazing down as I do everyday from this part of the Universe, the embarrassment which each of the seven players on Larkin's Lot went through would have broken the courage of Geronimo. It would have tested the strength of Superman. It would have tried the soul of Mother Teresa herself.

It would even have destroyed the confidence of that most famous of Irish football coaches, the Man Himself. That tells you how bad it was.

So is it any wonder that things turned out the way they did? Is it any wonder that they decided that they didn't want to lose any more? Is it any wonder that they wanted their dreams to come true and that they made the choice that they did? After all, they were just humans, like all the rest of you reading this. So why shouldn't they want their world to be just a little better?

But I'm ahead of myself again. Let me get back to the story. The trouble really started with that first match. And from there ... well, it was one long, loooonngg slide into oblivion and sure hell-fire ...

'Run. Run!' Gerry Larkin ran, panting, trying to get

out in front of the ball far enough so that he could get a clear shot out to Big Jimmy. He didn't know what he was doing back here. This was defence country. The Bright Brothers should have been on the ball, but the Bright Brothers didn't seem to know where they should be positioned. Instead, Gerry, playing striker, found himself with the ball a good twenty metres into his own side of the pitch.

'Get out there, Jimmy!' he screamed, motioning Big Jimmy into an open space between George Smith and Richard Markey. The big fellow tried to fake. He moved a step to his left, and ran straight into Wilder who was coming in to cover the open area. Wilder hit the big tub of charging fat like a horsefly striking a speeding Mini. Larkin could almost hear the 'splat'. He was amazed at the power of the large, determined, running figure that was Big Jimmy. So what if he was slower than a snail on a warm day? With his size, who was counting?

For at least the fifth time that day, Gerry Larkin fed him the ball. The shot, for a change, was perfect. The idea, thought of quickly right before the match, was to get the ball up the pitch to Big Jimmy, at which point he would feed back to Gerry, who in turn would try to get the quick shot into goal.

Unfortunately, the plan wasn't working too well. For one thing, Gerry was always forced out of position by the incredibly poor play of the Bright Brothers and Tommy Reynolds. He couldn't blame Tommy too much, of course. Tommy had forgotten to bring his elasticated glasses strap along to the match, which meant that he couldn't wear his specs, which meant that he couldn't see. Gerry, running down the field with the ball, looked over to see where Tommy was. His team-mate still stood in the centre of the pitch, eyes squinting out in all directions, looking for the ball - which was now moving at speed away from his general direction of view. As Gerry watched, he heard Fran, playing keeper, yelling, 'Tommy! Turn around! The ball's over there! Open your eyes. Over there!' Gerry could only sigh in disbelief.

The Bright Brothers, on the other hand, were turning into an unbelievable model of ineptitude. The twins had decided on a defensive strategy which Larkin suspected had never before been played in the history of football. Not anywhere in the world. Almost took the left-hand side of the field. Not Quite the right-hand side. Together, they would squirm up and down the sidelines like a matching set of runaway goldfish, running up toward the McNamara team goal, then back toward the Larkin's Lot team goal. Up and back; back and up. It was a good strategy - if you could ignore the fact that their movements had nothing whatsoever to do with the position of the ball.

Larkin screamed at them time and again to get back in position, but they chose to ignore him or forgot or became confused. Whatever the reason, they weren't really there. Effectively, Larkin's Lot only had five members on its team ...

... five scared, inept, rather uncertain players playing against seven of the most vicious, back-biting, ignorant, unrepentant footballers they could hope to play against: McNamara's Death Squad. And this was only their first match.

Larkin turned the ball awkwardly. Big Jimmy, having just polished off Wilder, turned signalling for the ball. Larkin's foot struck. The ball flew above the wildly swinging defensive arms of George Smith. It's perfect! Gerry thought, watching as the ball arced toward the plodding big man. All that Big Jimmy had to do was turn and finish it into the gaping net. Already, McNamara - playing keeper - was coming out of position toward the ball. If Big Jimmy could just concentrate, they'd score!

... which, of course, wasn't meant to happen. Big Jimmy, having signalled for the ball, turned his back on Gerry, gazing viciously at McNamara. McNamara - no one's fool - took one look at the horrifying tonne of fat coming his way and moved casually to the side. This goal I'll let them have, McNamara thought. While scaring McNamara to death, however, Big Jimmy forgot one thing - to look behind him for the ball. So, when Gerry kicked his beautiful pass, all that faced the ball was Big Jimmy's huge flapping backside. The ball went up. The ball came down - hitting the big fellow smack in the middle of his ample posterior.

What happened next came to be pretty much the expected thing for Larkin's Lot.

The ball popped off Jimmy's backside, ricocheting like a deflated beach ball into the head of Harold Smyth, who was trying his best to keep out of the way. Upon being hit, Harold folded like a drunken scarecrow, falling to earth on the flat of his back, his eyes immediately filling with a pint of tears. There he waited, feeling sorry for himself - until he looked up to find the enraged might of the McNamara team descending toward him like a swarm of enraged hornets. He didn't understand why he should be the focus of their lethal attack, until he finally realised that the football had become lodged beneath both of his legs. Urgently, sensing impending doom, Harold tried to kick the ball loose, but only got tangled in the long pink T-shirt that his sister had lent him, and which was the only T-shirt available to him on the day.

The McNamara defensive consignment - Alan Wilder (finally back into play, but still trying to shake off the clobbering that he had received from Big Jimmy), Richard Markey and Larry O'Shay, all came running in toward the unprotected target which was Harold Smyth, not caring if the poor kid got pummelled in the process.

Harold screamed sharply and drew his body into a foetal position - legs and head drawn up into his quivering belly - which probably saved his life. The ball popped loose, shooting down the pitch, to be intercepted there by Clay Barkley, the McNamara team forward, who had been waiting for just this kind of opportunity.

Clay was positioned near midfield and ran right past blind Tommy Reynolds. Reynolds, sensing that action was at hand, but not being able to see a thing, put out both arms clumsily. Clay, now dribbling the ball downfield at full steam, never had a chance. He took both arms across the chin, a tremendous, crippling stroke that dropped him like a slaughtered bull. Tommy, not knowing that he had made a decisive - though illegal - play, stood there, puzzled, wondering what had hit his outstretched arms. The ball, still rolling from Clay's last touch, ran right between Tommy's spread-eagled legs.

In that this was not professional football, the teams did not have the help of a referee to call 'Foul!' at such a stroke of gross ineptitude. This meant that Tommy stayed on the field and Clay, trying to determine if he still had a head, remained flat on his back.

Now, all that was between the ball and the goal was Fran. Gerry could see her get ready; crouching down in her Do or Die defensive pose, spreading her weight evenly on both legs, waiting for the McNamara team attack. He couldn't let her down, he knew. Somebody had to help.

He searched wildly for the Bright brothers, but their prancing strategy was mistimed: they were now at the far end of the pitch. Gerry, realising that his screams were being ignored, turned back toward the ball, now a good thirty metres upfield.

Gunner Barkley, playing striker, had watched his brother Clay get the stuffing knocked out of him, and was now bent on revenge. He also noticed that he was in a perfect position to do something about it. Quickly, he ran forward on his strong, athletic legs, intercepting the ball as it rolled slowly away from his still-dazed brother. Gunner gave it a quick flick into the centre of the field, running up behind it. Fran, watching him like a young, uncertain hawk, knew what she had to do. She put her head down, and ran out of the keeper's box like a mini-rocket.

Gerry Larkin knew that he had only one choice.

With all of his other team members either on the ground, blind, or out of position, he ran like a mad, crazed puppet down the pitch, screaming at Frances to get back into the box.

Hearing the scream, Gunner Barkley turned in confusion. He was between the charging madman and Fran Clifford. To stay there, unconcerned, would - he knew - be an act of insanity. Larkin, never known for his coordination, might very well run right over him.

Gunner Barkley stopped dead, holding the ball easily on his left toe. He looked back at the human locomotive careening downfield, and grinned. With a deft movement, he tossed the ball easily into the air, at the same time stepping to the right, out of harm's way.

Gerry Larkin suddenly saw the bulk of Gunner in front of him. He decided to put the brakes on, but it was too late. The pounding legs, hearing the orders from Gerry's mind, became suddenly confused. They over-reacted, and Gerry found himself tumbling head over heels toward the net.

Fran, now seeing her team-mate hurtle toward her, did what she could to get out of the way, but it wasn't enough. She tried to duck, but the steamroller which was Gerry Larkin's infinitely long arms, feet and hands caught her, drawing her into their dangerous suction like a giant food processor. When it was finished, the two of them were tied together like a huge piece of confused human spaghetti ...

... the ball, meanwhile, completed its slow rise into the air and plopped directly in front of

Gunner's foot, just where he had intended. Insolently, he rolled the ball around the heaving mass of the human accident, and rolled it softly, contemptuously, into the Larkin's Lot net.

One-nil. Gunner grinned evilly. 'And this!' he shouted, punching the sky with a closed fist in vile victory, 'is only the beginning!' Unfortunately for Larkin's Lot, he was right. For the remaining minutes of the match, Larkin's Lot played like the group of misbegotten, unwanted, untalented, unconfident woebegone players they thought themselves to be. They could have been playing ice-hockey, for all anyone cared. And it was true that they seemed as if they were playing on ice. They slipped, fell, slid, tumbled, scrambled and otherwise careened through the rest of the match without once making a decisive threat on the McNamara net.

By five o'clock, and the end of the match, the score was twelve-nil. Twelve-nil! The seven of them, all war-weary veterans of the great pounding, sat on the sodden ground, the echoes of McNamara's Death Squad jeers still revolving in each of their shattered brains. Gerry, taking in great gulps of air to steady his shaky lungs, couldn't believe that they had played so poorly. He knew that they would probably be beaten - and soundly, but twelve-nil?

'That's all right,' Fran said confidently. 'We'll do better next time.'

Gerry, sitting on his backside in the damp grass, could only stare at her, shaking his head with certainty. 'There isn't going to be a next time.'

The rest of the team, surrounding him, agreed. 'We play like that again,' Big Jimmy stated, his triple chin quivering like mushy jelly, 'we'll get laughed out of the county.'

But Frances Bernadette Mary Therese Clifford - always the optimist - wouldn't quit. She shifted her tiny figure on to the balls of her feet, and thrust her small chin out fiercely. 'It's only the first match. Only the first! You just wait and see. Things will get better!' she informed them in her tough voice.

But Gerry, now trying to shake out the cramps in his giraffe-like legs, didn't think so. Tommy Reynolds spoke up, saying what they all thought. 'This,' he said with a studied voice, 'is going to be a very long season.'

And so the rest of the school year moved past in miserable monotony. Larkin's Lot played ten more matches, each match worse then the rest. They played against St Mary's (score: fourteen-nil). Then against Mercy Convent (score: seventeen-nil). Then the all-girl school at St Therese Secondary (score: nineteen-one. At least they had managed to score through a monumental stroke of luck when four of the Therese Secondary team became absorbed in a moving discussion of this week's adventures of *Brookside*.)

The scores got worse and worse.

Schools from all over the county now asked them to play. They asked, knowing that by playing they were certain not only of an easy win, but also knowing that they would experience the most hilarious, ridiculously inept football that it would

40

ever be their pleasure to watch. Larkin's Lot was entertainment on a grand scale. Better, even, than a half-hour of *Neighbours* or *EastEnders*.

Larkin's Lot had become the joke of the county, and Gerry, Fran, Big Jimmy and everyone else knew it. It was embarrassing. Insulting. Painful. And the fact that they were playing football no longer seemed to be the big deal that it once was.

All that the seven of them understood was that they were tired of losing. They were tired of the laughter from the other teams. They were tired of the teasing and annoying little remarks made by friends at school. The end came when they had been decisively beaten twenty-seven-nil by St Frances Xavier. That was the end of it. The very end. The laughter from the Xavier audience (thirty-four kids and three dogs had come along to enjoy the fun) had started at the beginning of the match. It had risen as Larkin's Lot wandered like a group of disorganised circus clowns all over the pitch. It had reached a crescendo when Big Jimmy, doing his best to keep a wayward ball in play, had inadvertently run straight down the field, knocking the Xavier keeper on his behind. Steaming on like an out of control cannon-ball, arms windmilling as he tried to stop his momentum, Big Jimmy continued on - forever on - right into the Xavier goal, tearing the poor thing to pieces, net, frame and all.

Thus came the last, final, and most humiliating defeat to be suffered by Larkin's Lot.

At the end of the Xavier match, the seven team members sat on the grass miserably, waiting for the axe to fall, finally, on their dreams.

'This is terrible,' Tommy Reynolds said, cleaning his glasses absently.

'Ridiculous,' Harold stated weakly.

'I feel like an ambulance case,' Big Jimmy added as he gently explored the bruise - as large as a Florida orange - that now adorned his large, slick head, the result of his encounter with the goal.

'You look like an ambulance case,' Almost Bright countered sourly. 'And dead on arrival, at that.'

Big Jimmy glanced at him threateningly. Big Jimmy could cream any member on his team - or any other team, for that matter - if he had half a mind to. He thought for a moment of crushing the creep into a pancake, then realised that the idiotic figure of Almost Bright wasn't worth the effort. 'Watch it, Erasurehead,' he said instead, waving a fat fist like a mallet. 'You're this close to death.'

In response to the threat, Almost Bright stuck out his tongue, thinking somehow that Big Jimmy would ignore this further small display of courage. But Big Jimmy, seeing the wet pink tongue wave like some sort of obscene serpent, and with the sting of yet one more crushing defeat still ringing in his ears, had had enough. He rose, the lard on his waist sloshing around like a sickening tide, and stood menacingly directly over Almost.

Almost, suddenly realising that his life was in peril, started to scream. At which point, Not Quite - having taken off his football boots and engaged in picking his toenails clean with a dirty thumb - decided that it was his duty to protect his twin brother, no matter what the physical consequences.

He hurtled through the air at Big Jimmy, colliding with the tub of fat at its most vulnerable point - just below the knees. Big Jimmy, stunned for a moment at the sudden surprise attack, collapsed like a sack of potatoes. Unfortunately for the Bright brothers, Big Jimmy's tonne of fat sloshed over the two of them, pinning both firmly to the ground.

'Get off!' Almost gasped, suddenly aware that he was going to die of suffocation.

'Mmmffpphhhss!' Not Quite agreed. He had fallen on his face, and was tasting the not too appetising flavour of Mother Earth. 'MMMff-pphhSS!' he said again, more urgently. If Big Jimmy didn't get up, Not Quite knew that he would be ground into a permanent feature of the Xavier football field.

Gerry Larkin and Fran Clifford, who were sitting at distant ends of the pack of seven team players, both realised that they would have to do something if they wanted to stop a double murder.

'Come on, Jimmy. Get off of 'em,' Gerry stated, not wanting to get up. He was still winded from the match and angry at yet another loss. Gerry Larkin looked over at Big Jimmy, still plopped on the two Bright brothers, wishing that they would all just go away and leave him in humiliated peace. Big Jimmy, knowing that he had both of his tormentors exactly where he wanted them, wasn't sure that he wanted to move. Instead, he turned his head to Gerry, a big smile plastered on his cue-ball face.

Gerry sighed deeply. 'Look,' he said, getting a bit mad, 'if you stay there, you're going to kill 'em.'

Big Jimmy could only grin. 'So what about it? If I

kill 'em, I'd be doing the world a service.'

'Do what he says, lard face.' Fran, who had watched the exchange, decided to get into the act. She was also feeling terrible because of the loss, but it was still her team, after all. And the Bright brothers were two of their players. She couldn't just sit there waiting for them to die of suffocation.

The smile on Big Jimmy's face disappeared. 'What did you call me?' he said to Fran, his large voice growing suddenly very quiet.

'I said, get off them,' she repeated. Fran stood up suddenly and marched over to the downed bodies. She stood over them, hands on hips, confronting Big Jimmy like a captain taking stock of a beached whale. 'You don't get off 'em by the time I count to five, and you'll just have to take the consequences.'

Big Jimmy couldn't believe that this small fry would even consider making threats. He looked up at her, menacingly. 'These guys ...' he pointed a fat thumb toward the flattened bodies lying under his considerable belly, ' ... were making fun of me. Now get out of here before I pack you in here like another sardine.'

Fran stood watching him, danger in her eyes, considering her next move. Gerry still sitting on the ground, could not believe that she would put her life on the line so easily. Slowly, he stood up, readying himself for mortal combat.

Fran Clifford looked down on the beady eyes of Big Jimmy and said slowly, 'You are one of the fattest. Slowest. Most inept. Most repulsive. Football players. I have ever. Seen. IN MY LIFE!'

At which point, Big Jimmy could only see red. He

reached up with a pudgy hand, grabbing Fran by the ankle, smashing her to the ground as easily as an elephant swatting a mouse, and twice as fast.

Gerry saw it, and launched himself, all five foot eight inches of gangling appendages, toward the fray. Tommy Reynolds, realising that it was death before dishonour, joined the now-whirling pile of arms and legs, stopping only long enough to place his glasses gently on the freshly mowed grass.

Harold, meanwhile, figuring that one more body wouldn't really make a difference, and deciding that it was much better to live to fight another day, sat quietly on the sidelines keeping score.

The six players fought and kicked and bit and screamed and spat and pulled and attempted to mutilate the other five who were caught up in the maelstrom. They fought because they were angry. They fought because they were exhausted. They fought because they were frustrated.

But most of all, they fought because they were tired of losing.

For fifteen minutes, the team - except Harold - kept it up until they couldn't keep it up any more. Their arms, swinging at each other raggedly, started to feel like lead weights. They gasped like a line of ancient motor cars ready to call it quits.

Finally, Gerry Larkin, tired of the battle ... tired of football ... tired of losing, stood up in the centre of the still-moving mass of people and shouted to the sky, 'I don't care if the Devil himself has to help us! I JUST WANT TO WIN!'

Unfortunately, someone who would manage to help them do just that was coming toward them.

Chapter Five

'You called?' it said.

Gerry Larkin, standing in the pile of still-fighting team-mates, startled by the booming voice coming from behind him turned suddenly, almost losing his balance. He stood there, gaping into space at the figure that he now saw, while his so-called friends still tried to beat each other into pulp. He swallowed hard, and opened his mouth. Nothing came out but a small gag which sounded more like a dying tortoise than a voice. Gerry's mouth opened and closed a couple of times, sort of flapping in the breeze. Then he got some control and managed to make some noise.

'Fran,' he whispered in a small voice. He shook his large head, trying to get the vocal chords working better. 'Fran?' he said, just a little louder. He looked down. He saw a mud-covered leg which he knew was Fran's. It was just visible under the web-lock of legs and arms of the other Larkin's Lot players, and he reached down, hauling her pint-sized body up and out of the general hubbub.

'FRAN!' Gerry Larkin now yelled, trying to get her attention. Fran Clifford was still fighting mad, even if she was exhausted.

'What?' She spun toward him, breathing hard, her hands balled up into tiny fists, ready to sock him if he made a false move. 'What? What Do You Want, Larkin?' she breathed out threateningly.

Gerry Larkin nodded at the thing behind her. 'I think you'd better see this,' he managed. Then, abruptly, he sat down on the damp ground. Fran Clifford turned, and stood stock-still, and for a moment Gerry Larkin thought that she had turned to stone or concrete or something ...

... Fran Clifford looked at the presence that appeared in front of her and almost passed out. She knew, of course, exactly who it was. She had read about it in almost every horror book that she had ever had the occasion to glance through. Then, of course, there were the Bible references to it in her religion classes, and the stuff that she had seen in the films. Of course, usually you didn't see it, she thought. Usually, they just referred to it. Sort of indirectly. As if they were afraid to mention it.

But now, Fran Clifford knew what it looked like. And she didn't like what she saw at all.

It stood there in front of her in a sort-of haze, as if it hadn't managed to put all the fires out. The smoke coiled up around it, hiding its face one moment, its arms the next, its body the next - then suddenly clearing as if a giant electric fan had been switched on.

Its legs were huge, ugly and scaled. Like a giant reptile's. The feet were just as large - larger, she thought. The toe-nails were sticking out, so long that they curled upwards in full circles.

The arms and chest were hairy. Strong and powerful like a wrestler's, she thought. She suddenly wondered how it would do if it was entered into Wrestle-mania, then managed to put the thought away and concentrate.

But it was the face that got to her. The head with its huge ears. Smooth and slimy. Like a salamander's. And the two small, needle-like horns thrusting up from the skull like some sort of evil antennae, just where she knew they would be. Then there were the gigantic wings, their sickening, leatheriness folded against its sides. But the most frightening bit, the most sickening part of its entire, leery countenance, was the tail ... the coiling tail with the small spike on the end. A tail that coiled and reared like a mindless snake, thrashing the ground behind it ...

... but finally, there were the eyes. The golden eyes. Like a snake's. Glinting in the narrow face. She looked into those eyes for a moment, and wanted to scream ...

Meanwhile, the other team members had just about had enough of their wrestling match. They were exhausted. Big Jimmy, now flat on his back where the others had managed to turn him, had both of the Bright Brothers (still spitting dirt from their mouths, but knowing wisely that they were lucky to be alive) straddled across his ample belly. Tommy Reynolds had dragged himself clear of the mass of humanity and sat polishing his glasses.

And Harold Smyth, having grown bored with the whole thing, had long ago forgotten to keep score. But now, they all felt - rather than heard - the presence of what was before them. And without being told to do so (some things, you just know about) they turned to look, and each jaw dropped and all they could do was stare in horrified wonder at the thing which stood before them.

It stood watching them with its leering smile, puzzled for a moment at their rather stupid-looking astonishment. Then, it glanced down, taking a long look at its rather disturbing appearance.

'Oh, sorry!' it said suddenly. 'Didn't mean to frighten you.' It raised a long arm, and the entire team moved back in unison, thinking it was about to hit them with a hex or a ball of fire or some other hellish weapon. However, it simply waved a hand - a hand featuring incredibly long, webbed fingers and disturbingly sharp nails, in the air.

'Now,' it said, looking up at them again. 'Is that better?'

And where there had once been standing the beast of each of their individual nightmares, now stood a man. Just a man. Dressed simply - almost elegantly - in a dark suit and bow-tie. A large brimmed hat was stuck jauntily on top of the waxed coal-black hair. He held a walking stick lightly in white-gloved hands.

To be honest, he looked like something out of a 1950s television programme.

Larkin's Lot blinked as one person.

'What's the matter?' he said, jauntily. 'Devil got your tongue?' He sniggered lightly, the great jokester.

None of the team answered. They couldn't answer. You could have driven a herd of elephants through the silence and no one would have been able to say a word.

Finally, Fran Clifford managed to get her set of

jaws working. She pointed at him. 'You ...' she said, through chattering teeth. 'You ... you ... you ...' She couldn't say anything else. She sounded like a freight train chugging in toward its last stop.

He pointed at himself, suddenly all charm. 'Me?' he said smoothly. 'Oh, dear! I forgot to introduce myself.' He pulled an embossed business card suddenly from the air. He hadn't been holding it before. He hadn't reached into a pocket to get it. He just pulled it from the air. He handed the glinting card to Fran, who took it with quivering hands. 'Allow me to start the introductions. I ...' At which point, a phone began ringing. He sighed deeply in frustration, this time reaching into his suit pocket. From the depths of his coat, he pulled a standard-looking mobile telephone. 'Sorry,' he said apologetically. 'Work, work, work!' and he pressed the call answer button.

In the interlude, Fran looked at Gerry. Gerry looked at Fran. 'Do you know who that is?' he whispered to her.

'Do you think I'm stupid or something? Of course I know who it is,' she whispered back hotly.

Gerry swallowed thickly. He felt as if he might puke, he was that scared. 'Don't you think we should run or something?' he said shakily.

'Hah!' Fran replied impatiently. 'Do you really think we can run from him? Didn't you see how he pulled this card,' she held the business card under his nose - it smelled faintly of sulphur, 'right out of thin air? I don't think running is going to solve anything,' she whispered hoarsely. 'We're just going to have to sit tight and see what this is all about.'

She glanced around her. The rest of the team were still frozen into position on the ground. It looked as if they had all died and rigor mortis had just set in. This, in turn, reminded her that their new visitor might just have death on his mind. She tried to turn off this line of thought before it became any more frightening, and looked again at the sprucely dressed gentlemen who was now finishing his telephone call.

'Look,' he was saying, 'I don't care what they say. You just tell them that I said that I want this job done *now*!' He smiled up at Gerry and Fran, indicating with his glinting gold eyes to hold on, this was only going to take a second more. 'Adolf. Adolf. Shut up! Now you listen to me. I'm in a meeting. You get those people back to work down there. I want it hotter than ...' he stopped himself abruptly, glancing at the team apologetically as he found another word, '... Hades down there before I get back. We've lost at least three hundred degrees in the past two months, and you're going to have to get it back up to scratch. Either that or ...' he lowered his voice, threateningly, ' ... or you're going to find yourself in a much *warmer* job. Do we understand each other?' He pushed a button on the telephone, cancelling the call.

'That Adolf. Can't seem to take directions,' he said in frustration. 'I can't figure it out. He ran the entire German army during the Second World War. You'd think he'd have some management ability. But try to get him to stoke a little coal, and is he up to it?' He shook his head. 'Not at all! All he does is complain. Now,' he said, somewhat confused by the

51

change of subject, 'where was I? Oh,' he turned to them, again smiling warmly, and trying his best to wind himself back up into some sort of enthusiasm. 'The introduction. As I was saying ... my card.' He pointed to the business card which Fran held between her trembling fingers. She glanced down at its embossed lettering.

She read out loud, 'Lucky Lucy, Talent Scout.' She glanced back up at him, uncertain. 'Talent scout?' she said rather lamely. She had already seen Lucky Lucy as he really looked. He didn't look like a talent scout.

'Well,' he said defensively, 'that's what I call myself, anyway.' He smiled at Fran like a snake hypnotising its dinner. Lucy stretched out his arms, seeming to hold the entire world in his large embrace. 'I search the globe, ' he stated, 'looking for just the right candidates to join my team. And let me tell you,' he stared at Fran with his glinting eyes, 'not just anyone will do. They have to be just so!' he said, emphasising his point with a raised finger.

Gerry shook his head decisively. 'I'm not interested,' he said flatly. 'I don't care what you're offering. I have some idea of what you're trying to sell, but no way.'

'Now just you wait! Hear me out!' Lucky Lucy grinned warmly. 'I've got an absolutely guaranteed, show-stopping deal for you good people.' He turned to face the rest of Larkin's Lot. The five other team-members, still shocked by the frightening, amazing transformation of Lucky Lucy, tried to dig themselves into the wet grass of the pitch. 'And this deal is good for each one of you!' he said.

Fran, thinking perhaps Lucky wasn't going to swallow them up in a ball of hell-fire just yet, breathed deeply, trying to get her wits back. She knew that she shouldn't even talk to this thing. What little she could remember of her Sunday schooling belted through her mind. The Devil, she remembered, is Not to Be Trusted. Period.

Yeah sure, she thought. But Fran Clifford was curious. She was always curious. And now she wondered why Lucky Lucy would have come to see them, of all people.

She cleared her throat, looking at Gerry warningly. 'So, what's this deal you're talking about?'

Gerry started to say something. Fran growled at him threateningly. 'Hear the man out,' she said. Gerry decided to keep his mouth shut, thinking that if the Devil didn't get him, Fran might. And he didn't know which one would be worse.

Lucky Lucy smiled and bowed slightly. 'I see that the lovely lady has some manners. And I appreciate it! Now, let me tell you why I've come to see you ...'

'This better be good,' Almost Bright whispered.

Big Jimmy punched him in the stomach. 'Shut up, mop-head,' he said dully. 'Let the fellow speak.'

Lucky smiled slightly at the interruption. 'I'm certain that you'll all be pleased with what I have to say.' Lucky reached up, tipping his hat to a jauntier angle. 'I've been following you for weeks, now. Weeks!' He laughed wildly. 'You really like playing football, don't you?'

Gerry nodded slightly. 'Sure we do. I guess that's why we formed the team. We call ourselves ... '

'Larkin's Lot!' Lucky grinned again. 'Oh you don't have to tell me! I know all about you!'

The members of the team looked puzzled. 'How do you know all about us?' Fran asked.

'Oh, I have my ways, let me tell you.' Lucky began pacing, suddenly all business. 'Now, here's what I've observed.' He held up a manicured hand. Fran blinked, wondering where the white gloves had gone.

'One,' he said. 'You set up your own team because no one else would let you play.'

Fran nodded a little. 'True.'

'Two. No one would let you play because ...' Lucky put a hand over his mouth, trying not to laugh, 'none of you is any good! In fact, you're all lousy. You stink!' He started to giggle violently, gasping for air, holding his sides, the laughter now coming in huge heaves.

'You're so bad that ... HA HA ... people come just to watch you make ... make ... FOOLS of yourselves! You're better entertainment than any movie. Funnier slapstick comedy than Abbot and Costello! By Hades! You even put Laurel and Hardy to shame! HA! HA! HA!' Lucy had fallen on to the ground, tears running down his face.

'Oh, it's too good!' he gasped, trying to control himself. 'Too bloody marvellous!'

'That's not true!' Fran almost shouted, getting annoyed. She turned to Gerry, hands on her hips. Gerry saw that look on her face. He knew that she was getting angry, and he thought he should try to keep her temperature down to 'Mild'. If not, there would be an explosion, and Gerry didn't know what would happen if you let the Devil have it.

'Look, Fran, he's right.' He gazed down at Lucky, still howling with laughter. 'OK, so we're not very good. So what's the big deal?'

'Not true!' Fran shouted. 'Not! Not! Not!'

Gerry gazed to the heavens, feeling a rush of blood well up into his embarrassed face. 'Don't lie, Fran. We're not great. You don't have to lie about it.'

Lucky, still gasping on the ground, waved a finger weakly into the air. 'Oh, I don't mind lies! Not me of all people,' he said, trying to bring his laughter under control. 'But I'd better warn you. I always know the truth. And I have to tell you ...' His mouth started to quiver again. 'Larkin's Lot has to be the worst team in the history of football!' He clenched his sides again, and started laughing all over again, a horrendous river of laughter. 'And the funniest thing of all ... HAR HAR HAR ... is that you *don't have any idea just how bad you are*!'

Fran frowned angrily. 'OK, OK. We're terrible. So what about it?'

Lucky got up on his knees and hands, crawling toward her, the laughter still coming. 'Which,' he said, trying to control himself, 'brings me to point *three*. Your team has played, what? Ten matches this season? Is that right?' Lucky's chin was quivering this time. He put a hand on it, trying to hold it shut and losing the battle.

'Yeah, yeah. That's right,' Fran replied thickly.

Lucky raised his thin eyebrows. 'And tell me, you little people,' he giggled, 'how many of those matches have you won?'

Fran was getting angry. 'You seem to know

everything,' she humphed. 'You tell us.'

'None! None! None!' Lucy shouted with glee. Then he fell over on his side, and started laughing all over again.

Now the rest of the team were getting angry. Big Jimmy stood up, his fat sloshing a little less confidently than usual, and thumped over toward the oily-looking talent scout. He stood over the quivering mass of Lucky Lucy, looking down on him dully, the mountain of fat not sure if he could squash the little snake and get away with it.

'So what, reptile face?' Jimmy said slowly. 'We're a bunch of losers. So what ya going to do about it?'

Lucky Lucy stopped laughing. Slowly, he stood up. His golden eyes narrowed into small slits. His thin, dry-looking lips curled into a snaky smile. He put out his small, well-formed hands, placing them confidentially on to Big Jimmy's huge shoulders.

'Because, my boy,' Lucy said smoothly, carefully forming his mouth around each syllable. 'I. Can. Make. You. WIN! And to turn you into winners,' he continued intensely, 'all you have to do is ...' He put a hand into the air. There was a blinding flash of light. The smell of sulphur. A pall of dense smoke. And there, in his neat hand, Lucky held a yellow piece of parchment paper. He grinned. 'Sign this!'

He held the yellow parchment out toward them. Fran took it carefully. And as she did so, she could feel her very soul quiver. Slowly, she looked at it.

It was a contract. A contract for their souls.

Chapter Six

'*No way*!' Gerry said sternly. 'No way, I said,' The seven of them were huddled on the grass. Behind them, they could watch Lucky Lucy pacing impatiently. Every now and then he glanced at his diamond-studded watch.

The slick salesman from the River Styx looked toward them. 'Made up your minds, my bright angels?' he asked, too sweetly.

Fran shook her head at him. 'No. You're going to have to give us five more minutes.'

He opened his mouth to say something and Fran could see a row of pointed teeth. She shivered, moving back a step. He closed his mouth with a slap, covering it with a hand. 'Sorry!' he said in a high-pitched voice. 'Dentures, you know,' he stated coyly. 'Even the best of people have them.' His voice sounded like the out-of-tune church organ Fran's mum played on Sundays. 'I'll leave you little pets be until you've made up your minds.' He stalked away, grumbling impatiently.

'So what are we going to do?' Big Jimmy rasped. He tried to take the glittering contract away from Fran with his ham-like fists. She snatched it away, gazing at it. The parchment was slightly burned around the edges, looking as if it had come directly from a four-alarm fire. But the lettering! She held it up to the sun, examining it carefully. The lettering glinted golden in the sunlight.

'Gold!' she whispered in awe. 'The contract is lettered in gold!'

Big Jimmy tried to grab it again. Fran held it just out of reach. 'Stay away from it, meat head. You'll get grease on it or something.'

'What's it say? Read it,' Almost Bright asked stupidly. Carefully, she started to read it out loud. 'OK,' she said, clearing her throat. 'Listen to this.' And Fran Clifford started to read the contract from Hell in a strangled voice.

'"We the undersigned ..." - that's us, Almost,' she explained with a croak. Almost nodded, his red head bobbing like a puppy's, ' ... "agree that we freely sign over all rights, both present and future and into in perpe - " ah ...' Fran struggled with the word. Lucky heard her.

'That's "In perpetuity!"' Lucky said impatiently.

She shot a face at him. 'Hey! I'm only in sixth class, mister. We haven't had that word yet.' Lucky tossed his eyes to the sky, seeming to implore for some non-visual help from the general direction of the stratosphere. Fran turned back to Almost. 'That means we agree to it forever.' She continued once again, ' ... "We agree that we freely sign over all rights forever to our Souls to the said Chief Benefactor, Lucky Lucy ..."'

'You mean Satan, don't you,' Gerry said in a worried voice. 'It's Satan. The contract should make that clear.' He stabbed the contract with a long finger. 'Why doesn't it say that? We have to understand what we're doing here!'

'Oh, shut it, Gerry. That's not what it says. It says,' she read again, '"Lucky Lucy".'

Lucy was running out of patience. He walked over to the close-packed team. 'Look, kids. Lady and gentlemen? I'm running out of *time*!' He turned to them. Gerry could see smoke drifting from both of Lucy's ears. Larkin cringed a little, waiting for a temper or two to snap. 'I have appointments all over the place. London. Washington DC. Dublin Castle. There are deals to be made all over the world! And I don't have time to mess around with these little ones.' He smirked at them. 'You know, you're not that big a deal.'

Fran glared at him. 'Oh yeah?' She thrust the glistening piece of paper toward the talent scout. 'If that's the case, then we don't want to even look at it.'

Lucy took a large breath and held it. Finally, when they thought he would pass out from lack of oxygen, he let go with an absolutely foul-smelling lungful of air. The team backed off two paces, trying not to gag.

Lucy tried hard to control himself. 'Fine,' he said, trying to control a tick that now crept into his left eye. 'I apologise. You're important! Take as long as you want to read it! I'll wait! Just sign it!'

Fran centred her small, compact gaze on him, her eyes narrowing. 'Look here, bud. I'm the team captain. You want us to sign the contract, we got to discuss it. Besides, we don't know what we get out of it.'

'What you get out of it? Oh, for ...' Lucy was about to explode, then thought better of it. He turned to them, his eyes falling for a moment on Gerry Larkin. Larkin felt as if he was going to fall through a hole in the ground under the slit-eyed gaze.

Lucky Lucy grinned suddenly. 'I know,' he stated, ringing his hands together in anticipation. 'How about a little demonstration? Sort of a trial run? That way, you'll know exactly how you'll all benefit by letting me be your agent.'

'What kind of demonstration?' Fran wanted to know.

Lucy pointed at Gerry Larkin. 'I'll allow Gerry here to show you all how it's going to be. And if you like it,' Lucy pointed at the contract, smiling sweetly once again, 'you sign. How about it?'

Fran thought about it. She couldn't see too much of a problem. She nodded her head once. Lucy smiled. He put out a hand, taking Gerry by the wrist. Gerry cringed at the touch. He wasn't at all sure that he wanted to be a guinea-pig for the Devil.

'Look, Fran,' he said, his eyes as round as squashed beetles, 'I don't think I want to ...'

Lucky interrupted him. 'And what was it that you, you giant,' he smirked, 'wished for?' Lucy thought for a moment, remembering suddenly. 'Oh, I know! You wanted to be a striker, didn't you? Well, a striker it is.'

Gerry opened his mouth to protest. He didn't have the time. Lucky Lucy clapped both hands over his head like a pair of evil cymbals. A peal of thunder crashed around them. The ground shook. The very air seemed to catch fire. Gerry Larkin stood in the centre of a personal maelstrom, black smoke curling around him, hoping that he was just imagining this. Hoping that he wasn't going mad ...

... and then, it stopped. The thunder ceased. The smoke cleared. The earthquake stopped its mad vibrations. Gerry Larkin stood, gaping. A glow of accomplishment emanating from Lucy's oily countenance. '*Voilà!*' he said. 'It is feenished!'

Gerry said, 'What's finished?'

'Oh, my friend! But you are different. Take my word for it,' Lucky said. Fran walked over to Gerry. The thunder and brimstone routine had scared her as well. She walked around Gerry, inspecting him carefully. Then she glanced at Lucky.

'He doesn't look any different,' she said.

'Oh, he's different all right.' He winked at Fran. 'Watch,' Lucky said simply. He pointed to a football which sat immobile on the grass. 'Kick it,' he said.

Gerry looked at Lucky suspiciously. 'No.'

Lucky's eyes narrowed, but Gerry wasn't going to give in. He wasn't going to take orders, no matter if it was from the Devil himself. Lucky glared at him. Then, as Gerry looked on, he saw twin pyres of smoke drift again out of Lucky's ears. Thick smoke, this time, like two Indian smoke-signals. Larkin decided that he'd rather kick the ball than be par-broiled by Lucky Lucy. He swallowed, feeling the Adam's apple bob up and down in his long neck.

'Okay,' he said unevenly. 'But don't expect much. Where do you want me to kick it?' he asked.

Lucky turned. Way out in the distance, maybe two or three hundred metres away, was a football goal. Lucky pointed to it. He smiled slowly. 'Kick it into the net, Gerry,' he said.

Gerry looked to where Lucky pointed. 'You're out of your mind!' his voice rising an octave. 'I couldn't even kick it half that far, much less get it into the net. Who do you think I am ...?' Gerry looked at Lucky, and decided to close his mouth.

Lucky had closed his eyes. Slowly he opened them. He gritted his teeth. 'Don't say another word, *Gerard*,' he stated flatly. 'Just *kick the ball!*'

Gerry Larkin thought that Lucky Lucy was going to explode. 'All right. I'll kick it.'

He took aim. He drew back his leg. He waited a moment, then thought, *Well, here goes nothing*.

He felt the contact with the ball - felt it like he had never felt anything before. The ball took off. Like an express train. Like a jet fighter. Like a bolt of football lightning.

Gerry Larkin gawked at the ball as it rocketed toward the net, watched as it arced purposefully, on target ... watched as it plunged now, through the unguarded opening, its power, even from this distance, sending the net into a mad tumble. Larkin had scored from over two hundred and fifty metres. A striker had been born. And what a striker!

Lucky Lucy turned to Frances Clifford. Fran's mouth hung open. Lucy swept around, gazing at them all. All of the team members' mouths were open. Not a sound could be heard.

'So!' Lucky Lucy said stubbornly. 'There's the proof. Now, as I said, I'm late.' He held out a pen, pointing at the contract. 'Sign!' he screamed.

Chapter Seven

'Blimey!' Gerry Larkin whispered. 'Did you see that?'

Fran nodded dumbly. 'How far is that?'

Tommy Reynolds came over. His glasses were foggy from the excitement. He took them off, wiping them slowly on his shirt, then put them on, measuring the distance to the goal. 'Two hundred and forty-three metres,' he said expertly.

'Did you see that?' Gerry Larkin said again. 'Holy Smoke -!'

'Shut up, Gerry.' Fran turned to the rest of the team. 'All right, lads. What do you want to do?' She held the contract in her hands, almost shoving it into their faces.

Big Jimmy grinned. 'I'll sign,' he said. 'I play forward, pal,' he intoned toward Lucky. Lucky smiled.

'Me too,' Tommy Reynolds said. He looked at Lucy. 'Midfield,' he stated with a smile plastered below his glasses.

The Bright twins were still gazing at the swinging football net. 'You mean you can make us all do that?'

Lucy nodded. 'Well,' he said, 'it depends. Your talent will be appropriate to your position. But let me tell you, you'll be the seven best football players in the world when I'm finished with you!'

Almost nodded. Not Quite nodded. They were in. 'Defence,' they said together.

'Count me in too,' Harold Smith whined. 'If the Bright twins can do it, I can do it too.' He sniffed loudly. 'Midfield,' he whimpered. Lucky Lucy nodded, glee in his eyes. He turned to Fran.

'And, Ms Team Captain,' Lucky stated. 'What about you?'

'Keeper,' she said.

'That's it!' Lucky shouted to the treetops. 'The New-Formula Larkin's Lot are about to be born!' He gazed at them. 'Oh, the fun you'll have. The glory you'll have! The number of teams you'll put out of business! The victories! It will be like nothing that you've ever known before! Now ...' his voice dropped an octave. From thin air, he produced the plain black pen again, '... all you have to do is sign. SIGN. SIIIIGGGGNNN!'

He handed the pen to Fran. She took it, studying it like a foreign immigrant. Finally, when she was sure, she brought the pen to the paper and ...

'I won't do it.' Gerry Larkin, still frightened at his sudden new talent, now watched the goings-on between Lucky and his team-mates with growing scepticism.

'What?' Fran said. 'What did you say?'

'What?' Big Jimmy said.

'What?' Tommy Reynolds said.

'WHHAAaaatt?' Lucky Lucy said, aghast. 'What do you mean, you won't do it?'

Gerry Larkin stood there, his arms crossed. He had had the time to think this through, and he wasn't going to sign. Not for his soul, he wasn't. He stood there, his five foot eight string-bean frame looking like a human exclamation point. 'No. I won't.' He marched over to Fran. He marched around the other five team members. 'Don't you understand what's going on here?'

'What's going on, ' Fran replied reasonably, 'is that we're about to become megastars.'

'HAH!' Gerry shouted. 'At what price?'

Fran glanced down at the contract she held. 'Not much,' she said matter-of-factly.

'Not much! Not much! This ... this ...' he pointed at Lucky, '... thing wants your souls, for God's sake.'

'Oh! That word!' Lucky said, cringing. 'Don't mention Him, if you don't mind. I get terrible headaches when He comes into the conversation.' Lucky put a hand to his head.

'See?' Gerry stated, as if this was all the proof he needed. 'This thing can't even stand hearing God's name, for God's sake!'

'Ohhhh,' Lucky moaned. 'My head.'

Fran shook her head. 'Stop being such a spoilsport. It's only a soul.'

'Only? Only?' Gerry shivered. 'Is that all you think it is? Don't you see? We'll all burn in Hell!'

Fran sniffed loudly. 'Hell - schmell,' she said. 'It's only a little heat. I hear it can be rather nice, as a matter of fact. And as for a soul?' She shrugged her shoulders. 'I mean, what's a soul? You can't see it, can you? You can't hear it or talk to it or eat it or take it out to dinner or have it over for a slumber party, can you? So what's the big deal? A soul seems kind of ... stupid ... if you ask me. I mean, it's worthless, you know? So why not trade it away?' She stood there looking at him.

Gerry shook his head. 'I don't believe you,' he said. 'I DON'T BELIEVE YOU CAN SAY THAT! What's a soul?' He turned, storming over to Lucky. 'Don't you know who this is?'

Fran nodded. 'It's the Devil.'

Lucky smiled. 'That's me, all right,' he said happily.

'Don't you know what he can do?'

'I don't know. Not much.'

'Oh I Give Up!' Gerry Larkin said, storming around and around, his long legs crossing then uncrossing. He finally got dizzy, he was storming around so much, and collapsed on to the grass. 'I don't believe you guys.'

Fran marched over to him. 'Look. You've been moaning and moaning about losing. What was the score against Xavier today? Huh?'

He looked at her glumly. 'Twenty-seven to -'

'To what? Twenty-seven to what, Gerry?'

He sighed. 'Twenty-seven to nil,' he said quietly.

'That's right! Twenty-seven to nil! Nothing! Nada! Are you proud of that, Gerry Larkin? Are you proud of losing?'

'No,' he mumbled.

'No,' she stated. 'So you're not proud of losing. And neither am I! or Tommy! or Harold! or any of the other team members!' She turned to the rest of the team. 'Am I right, gentlemen?'

'You're right!' they shouted.

'And now, here's our chance. Here's your chance. And what do you do? You moan about a little thing like a soul! I don't understand you.'

Gerry looked at her sullenly. 'Well, I don't care if you understand me or not,' he stated glumly. 'I'm not signing, and that's all there is to it.'

Fran shook her head sadly. 'You're a real loser, you know that, Gerry? A real loser.' She turned to the rest of the team, gazing at them. They looked at her expectantly. It was up to her now. Slowly, she walked over to Lucky. He stood, manicuring his nails absently in the sunlight.

'Well, we're just going to have to sign without Gerry,' she said.

Lucky blew on his highly polished nails. 'No can do,' he said simply.

'What?'

He smiled at her sadly. 'I'm sorry. Either I sign Larkin's Lot - and that means every one of you - or I sign nobody. Those are the rules.' He adjusted his bow-tie. 'Sorry,' he said, smiling.

'Aarrgghh!' Fran Clifford marched back over to Gerry Larkin. 'Did you hear him? Did you hear him? He won't sign any of us. Not without you!'

'So?'

'So! SO! Oh, God, I HATE LOSERS!' Fran turned her back on him.

The other team members glanced at each other. Slowly, they made their way over to Gerry Larkin. They circled around him, like a bunch of American Indians on the warpath. Big Jimmy reached down, grabbing him by the T-shirt, lifting him slowly to a standing position. The big fist tightened. Gerry suddenly realised that breathing was becoming rather uncomfortable.

'You going to sign or what?' Big Jimmy said.

'Let go!' Gerry gagged in a small voice. The grip got tighter. All that he could see was the glowering face of Big Jimmy. Gerry Larkin always thought Big Jimmy was ugly, but up close, he looked really ugly. 'I can't breathe!' he gasped.

'Good!' Big Jimmy stated.

'AAlllllrrrttt,' Gerry Larkin sputtered.

Big Jimmy smiled a little. His face looked rather like a happy hog's. 'What did you say?'

'Allllllrrrtt. Illll snnnn.'

Big Jimmy let go. 'Say it again so I can hear it.'

Gerry Larkin had both hands to his neck, massaging his crushed throat. 'I said I'll sign.'

'Good,' Big Jimmy said, turning away from him.

'On one condition.' Gerry Larkin looked at the team members standing there with murder in their eyes. He looked at Fran Clifford, his so-called friend. He looked at Lucky Lucy. 'I'll sign only if we get a six-months out clause.'

'A what?'

'A six-months out clause,' Gerry explained. The team members eyed him suspiciously. 'Look. A lot of professionals have 'em.' He pointed to the contract. 'We sign now. If, after six months from right now, we don't like it, the contract is torn up. We get our souls back. End of story.'

Lucky Lucy's face was aghast at the idea. 'Now hold on, young fellow. I never give an out clause ... '

'Just a minute,' Fran interrupted. She walked over to Gerry, studying his still gasping face. 'I like it. We get our powers for six months. At the end, we can then keep going with Lucky here,' she pointed

68

to Lucy, his mouth opening and shutting in quiet protest, 'or we quit! Seems simple enough.'

Lucky got his mouth working. 'No, no, no! That's not the way it's done! It's one way or the other ...'

'Look, salamander lips,' Fran stated, eyeing him coolly. 'You must want us pretty bad. Otherwise, you wouldn't have bothered to take the trouble on us. Isn't that right?'

Lucky didn't know what to say. He wasn't used to having anyone query his deals, least of all a pint-sized young woman. 'Well, ah, yeah. Maybe you're right. Maybe.'

'So, take it or leave it,' Fran said, crossing her arms stubbornly. 'We get the six-months out clause, or it's no deal.'

'I don't know what to say.' Lucky was trying to buy time. He didn't know what to do.

'It's called negotiating, Lucky. We're negotiating. Now take it or leave it,' Fran finished acidly.

'Oh ... ahhhhh ... all right!' He sighed deeply. 'What the heck. It's only one contract after all.' Lucky Lucy shook his head, and pointed to the contract which Fran still held. There was a flash. A smokescreen of black drifted up from the document. Fran looked at the contract again, studying it intently.

'It's here all right. See?' She pointed to the parchment paper. At the bottom it read,

NB. This is to amend the document. If after six months from today's exact time and date the parties to the first part - meaning Larkin's Lot - desire to end the contract with the Party of the Second Part - meaning Lucky Lucy

*- they can exercise this option, at which the Contract will
be deemed null and void.*

Signed,
Lucky Lucy

'There!' he sniffed. 'I hope you're satisfied now.'

Fran glanced at Gerry. 'Happy?'

He sniffed. 'No,' he said. Big Jimmy glared at him.
'But I'll sign,' Gerry finished hurriedly.

'Good.' She eyed the team. Her lips quivered,
raising into an immense smile. 'Let's do it.'

And each member of the team signed on the
dotted line. When they were finished, Fran handed
the contract back to Lucky.

'Good doing business with you,' he said, smiling
broadly. 'I'll be around, let me tell you. I think you'll
find that all your dreams will come true! Now, if
you'll excuse me, I must get on about my business.'
He turned to leave.

'Hey, lizard breath.' Big Jimmy stood there.
'Aren't you forgetting something?'

'Now what?' He slowly revolved back to face Big
Jimmy. 'And, pray tell, what could I have possibly
forgotten?'

'Our powers!' Big Jimmy stated. 'You know. Our
super fantastic football talent.'

'Oh, that.' Lucky glanced at him. 'You got that
when you signed the contract.'

'But what about the thunder and lightning and
everything?' Big Jimmy asked, his fat jiggling as he
talked. 'You know, like you did to Gerry?'

'Just pyrotechnics. A little showmanship, I assure

70

you.' He winked at Big Jimmy. 'You just go play football. You'll see that I've kept my end of the contract, just as stated.' A smile crept over his oily face. 'Now, if you'll excuse me?' He raised an arm. The ground shook. Lightning and thunder crashed.

And he was gone. As if he had never existed. All that was left was a copy of the contract, smoking slightly, lying on the spot where Lucky Lucy had disappeared so unexpectedly.

'Where do you think he went?' Not Quite asked.

'Where do you expect?' Fran answered crossly. She walked over, grabbing the contract. Turning, she eyed her other team-mates. Then, she put out a hand. 'See this?' she said. 'This is the hand of the *greatest keeper in the world!*'

Gerry Larkin laughed shortly. 'How do you know, Fran? How do you know that the whole thing wasn't just a joke? Or,' he thought, suddenly worried, 'what if he's taken our souls, and hasn't given us our powers?'

Fran smiled slowly. 'Oh, he's given them to us all right. And we're going to put them to the test.'

'How?' Tommy Reynolds asked, suddenly excited. 'How are we going to test them?'

Fran gave an evil grin. 'Tomorrow,' she said. 'McNamara's Death Squad. We'll take 'em on again. Only this time,' her face twisted into a smile as wide as a trombone, 'we're going to pulverise them!'

And the Larkin's Lot team screamed in delight. All except for Gerry, who just stood there, wondering if they hadn't been fooled by the greatest liar in the world ...

71

Chapter Eight

McNamara couldn't believe it when Fran Clifford rang him. He couldn't believe the crazies in Larkin's Lot would have the guts to play again. But that's what they wanted. And McNamara's Death Squad would accommodate suicide any time. Any time at all.

They met on the pitch after school. The seven ugly, menacing, unrepentantly vile members of McNamara's team stood off against seven members of Larkin's Lot. And around them, fifty schoolmates watched, grinning, waiting for the side-show to begin. 'Hey, maybe Larkin's Lot will get really creamed this time!' said one classmate.

'Naw. They're just going to get murdered!' said another. There was general laughter among the bloodthirsty crowd, and Larkin's Lot stood, waiting, feeling like animals on display.

For a while, the two teams just stood there silently, like deaf mutes waiting for the slaughter. McNamara snorted loudly, spitting a glob of greenish saliva in the general direction of Gerry Larkin. He grinned maniacally, playing up to the audience.

'You ready to get the tar beaten out of you again, laddie?' he said viciously.

Gerry Larkin gulped and shook his head

unsteadily on its long, giraffe-like neck.

'Nope. We aren't being beaten this time,' he said slowly, knowing that he really didn't believe what he said. Larkin couldn't believe it. Not yet. That said, he continued on with it anyway. 'It's you who's going to get beat this time, McNamara. You and your other slobs.'

'Huh? What'ja say, birdman?' McNamara started laughing and turned to Alan Wilder who was standing next to him. 'Ya hear that, Wilder? Ol' geek-man here says he's going to beat us.' McNamara turned back toward Gerry Larkin, and stomped toward him. He stood there, glaring into Gerry's scared face. 'Ain't nobody on your team going to beat us. You got that, geek?' McNamara hissed.

Gerry swallowed again. 'Ah, yeah. I got it.' McNamara smiled dangerously, then turned , stomping again back upfield. Gerry took a deep breath. He didn't care what Lucky Lucy had said. Lucky had probably lied to them, anyway. They probably didn't even have any amazing football skills. They were still seven scared, clumsy kids who were about to lose their next match.

He looked across at the seven members of McNamara's Death Squad. 'Wouldn't it be nice,' he said mostly to himself, 'to think that the deal with Lucky was real? That we really did have magical powers of some kind?' Thinking about it, he clearly remembered signing the contract. Maybe it meant something after all. No matter, he was still scared to death ...

Despite his shaking appendages, Gerry Larkin

cleared his fear-clamped throat. 'Except this time,' Gerry said. 'This time, we're going to get you, McNamara. I promise.'

The Death Squad captain spun around. He studied Gerry contemptuously. 'We'll see, Larkin. Let's play some football and find out!' And then the might of the Death Squad marched toward their positions, shouting murder as they went ...

'Right!' Fran shouted from her position in front of the net. 'You guys know what to do! Just do it!'

As one, the seven team members of Larkin's Lot nodded. As one, they watched as the ball was tossed high into the air. As one, they knew that this was it. This was the proof. This was the time to *know* that they were no longer misfits and losers. They were winners now! And by the Devil, they would play that way!

But rather than doing anything, Larkin's Lot stood there, watching the football as if it were an alien. Because they didn't want to play! How could they? What would happen if it all went wrong one more time!

And so, like spectators attending their own funeral, Larkin's Lot stood there and watched. And as they watched, their world started to fall apart. Again.

'What's the matter with you people?' Fran screamed. 'Play! Don't just stand there! Play!'

The ball jumped downfield, right past a whimpering Harold Smyth. Harold only stared at it. The ball continued, spinning toward Tommy Reynolds. Tommy took one step toward the ball, then stopped. It could have been a poisonous tarantula, he looked that frightened of it.

'Aaarrrgghh!!!' Fran bellowed, standing in the keeper's box. 'Do something!'

'Take it to them!' Gunner Bradley saw how scared they were. Larkin's Lot didn't seem to have any drive at all. He grinned wickedly. The ball breezed toward him unopposed. He grabbed it with a toe, turning it toward Almost Bright. All that Almost would do was back-pedal.

'Come on, Almost! Get the ball!' Fran screamed. Almost turned, shrugging at her in despair. As he did, Gunner dribbled the ball easily around Almost's inept feet. 'Thanks, idiot!' Gunner said, nodding at Almost insolently. 'Next time, try playing cards. It's easier.'

He was running now at speed down the field. He passed Not Quite Bright, standing there like an unused erasure. Not Quite watched him stupidly as Gunner passed him, his hair blowing in Gunner's slipstream.

Gunner turned around as he ran, waving his arms helplessly. Helpless, because he had started laughing uncontrollably. 'Hey, McNamara!' he called. 'Come on out here and help! These turkeys don't want to play!'

Gunner heard assorted laughter from upfield, and knew that his team-mates were now flowing toward him. But then, it dawned on him. Nobody was between him and the goal except Fran Clifford, and she didn't look exactly over-powering.

He stopped, turning back toward his team-mates. 'Don't bother,' he grinned. 'I think I can handle this one myself.' He rotated back downfield, gazing at Fran. 'Oh, Frances. Girlie, girlie. I'm coming to get you!' he smirked.

Fran swallowed. 'Well,' she said. 'Don't just stand there. Do something about it.' Gunner Barkley grinned again, and did as he was told ...

Ten metres out from the goal line, Gunner Barkley stopped suddenly. He gave Fran a sneering grin. 'So you're going to beat us, are you? Well, how's this to start things?'

She watched him, all of a sudden nervous. She knew that she had power - there was power in her somewhere! She looked at Gunner. She looked at him, but could do nothing! Nothing!

She watched as his large leg swung back, ramming viciously forward, WHACKING the ball towards her.

And all that Fran Clifford could do was duck. The ball rammed into the back of the net.

'One-nil! One-nil!' Gunner Barkley bellowed. He turned, running back down the pitch. 'Hey, McNamara! What was the worst score that Larkin's Lot had?'

'Twenty-seven-nil!' McNamara called, laughing, from in front of his own net. 'Against Xavier.'

'Oh yeah?' Gunner turned to the rest of his team-mates. 'What d'ya say, guys? Let's double it! How about fifty-four to nothin' when we finish with them?' McNamara's team started to hoot. The audience started to hoot.

'Losers! Losers! Losers!' they chanted. And as Gunner Barkley ran downfield, he threw his arm into the air, punctuating each shout of 'Loser!' with a sharp stab into a cloud-strewn sky.

Gerry Larkin watched it all. Heard it all. Heard the crowd going wild. Each cry of 'Losers!' seemed to drill into him, right into his heart. He felt as if he was being punched. The cries were socking him in the stomach. In the face. Punching into his very soul.

'Losers!' they cried. But Gerry Larkin wasn't a loser. He knew it. Deep down. And now, he knew that he could do something about it.

Gerry started to get mad. Really mad. He hadn't done a thing to help defend against Gunner's goal. Not a thing! It was his fault that they had scored, he knew. And because of not even wanting to test his new skills - because he was afraid that they might not exist at all - he didn't want even to try.

It dawned on him, drumming into his mind. As if someone ... something ... were there, whispering sweet things into his large cauliflower ear. 'You're not a loser, Gerard,' it whispered evilly. 'You can beat these guys. That's what I promised, remember?'

He shook his head roughly, feeling the anger come into him like a fire from Hell. And with the anger, he felt the power course up through his giraffe-like body, filling it with an energy so hot that he felt the grass would burn beneath his feet.

Gerry Larkin gazed back upfield at the hooting Gunner Barkley. He felt his eyes turn red. The anger boiling into them. 'Barkley!' Gerry Larkin barked. 'Shut up!'

Barkley, still running downfield, still shouting 'Losers!' put on the brakes. He turned, wondering who could have demanded such an order. 'Larkin?' he stated threateningly. 'Did you say something to me?'

'Darn right I did, wimp!' Larkin breathed. 'I'm mad, and I'm not a loser, and you're going to find out about it. RIGHT NOW!'

Gerry Larkin turned, then, and knew that he was about to play football!

'All right, team!' Gerry yelled. He had the ball between his two feet, standing in midfield. In front of him, the seven opposing players stood, leering at him, begging Larkin to make a charge toward the goal, begging Larkin's Lot to make a play at them because, undoubtedly, they would mess up.

And behind them, crowding around the pitch, shouting as if they were watching an execution, were the cheering fans. Cheering for the heads of Larkin's Lot and another fabulous loss! 'Losers! Losers! Losers!' they chanted.

Gerry Larkin turned, surveying his team. In back of him was Tommy Reynolds, looking expectantly through his thick glasses. The Bright Brothers stood there, the pair of them staring at Larkin like death-row victims waiting for a reprieve. Harold Smyth gazed woefully forward, hands in pockets, saying nothing - but it was so very obvious that he was tired of losing, too. Big Jimmy stroked his round head, looking anxiously at Gerry, waiting for orders.

And behind them all was Fran, standing in the goal, still smarting from Gunner Barkley's score. She looked blankly at Gerry Larkin. Waiting for him. Looking to him, finally, for courage and direction and faith in their devilish abilities.

Gerry Larkin felt the power in him, and knew that it was in all of them. 'Let's do it,' he half-whispered to himself. And then, like an evil miracle, Larkin's Lot started to play football.

Gerry dribbled the ball forward. Gunner Bradley stood, blocking his way. 'You're a loser, Larkin,' he snickered sickeningly. Gerry smiled at him slyly. He raised his head, faking right with the ball. He turned suddenly, spinning left. His mind was working! The ball followed his feet! Gunner Bradley stood there, moving awkwardly trying to cover the fake, then fell with a thump, tripping over himself.

Gerry flicked the round leather ball over to Tommy Reynolds. Reynolds took it. Dribbling it forward now, he was running, running down the field, the ball moving forward, right past an amazed Richard Markey. Reynolds didn't understand where the power had come from. He stopped suddenly, his glasses steamed with fright.

'Tommy! You can do it! Run!' Gerry ordered. And Tommy ran. He glanced toward the centre of the field. Big Jimmy had moved up into position. Ten metres in front of goal. McNamara saw him, the wide, hulking girth of flapping fat, and back-pedalled in toward the net.

Reynolds flicked the ball up into the air, bowling it cross field, in toward the net. The ball fell toward Big Jimmy, who sensed it coming down, now - right down toward him.

He looked McNamara squarely in the eye. And he grinned.

The ball hit the Big Man flat in the stomach. And

Big Jimmy gave a tremendous belch. The ball ricocheted right off the huge fat of his belly, powering past the outstretched arms of a surprised McNamara and into the net.

THEY HAD SCORED!

Gerry Larkin grinned wickedly. 'That's one, McNamara,' he said. 'And this is just the beginning.'

McNamara booted the ball. It sailed up, up - coming down into midfield. Clay Barkley put up his hand. 'I got it!' he screamed.

'No, you don't,' he heard from somewhere behind him. 'We've got it.'

The Bright Brothers swept by him like twin red locomotives. Clay Barkley had already committed himself. He had jumped high, but not high enough, as it turned out. Almost, jumping five feet into the air like a crimson pogo-stick, took the ball right off his head ... flicking it right on to the toe of Not Quite, who took the ball expertly, turning it, weaving upfield ...

... it all happened so fast for Clay Barkley. One minute the ball was there. The next minute ... space. Barkley went up. Barkley came down. Right on his well-padded backside. He looked upfield, shaking his head, not believing what he was seeing ...

... Not Quite roared ahead. Harold followed him two steps behind. In front of them stood Alan Wilder. Wilder was in no mood to let them through. Not after that first goal. But Wilder never had a chance.

Not Quite, charging toward him at full speed - stopped. Stopped like a piece of chewing gum hitting a window. 'Vwwoop!' He was stock still. And the ball had stopped with him ...

... Wilder, meanwhile, who had been charging toward him at speed, careened on and on ... like a charging rhino missing its target. He looked up just in time to see Big Jimmy - immovable Big Jimmy, standing suddenly in front of him, a great, unmoving mountain of animal flesh.

And Alan Wilder, still moving at speed, hit him at full tilt. Hit him like a cannonball colliding with a solid steel block. And as Wilder slid mercifully to the ground, all the lights went out ...

... the ball, meanwhile, was still beneath the rock-solid toe of Not Quite Bright who sensed, rather than saw, Harold Smyth come charging up behind him. Not Quite, staring now at a completely perplexed McNamara, stuck his tongue out at the Death Squad captain, and gingerly moved his toe away from the ball.

Harold Smyth, charging forward, struck the ball with all his might and watched it zip, now, right beside the stunned McNamara, into the top left-hand corner of the net. Harold Smyth looked, unbelieving, at the goal that he had just scored. 'I did it! I did it! I did it!' He charged downfield, into the outstretched arms of his team-mates.

McNamara, sitting on the ground, could only watch. 'What is going on? How did he do that?'

'Wouldn't you like to know?' Gerry Larkin said suddenly, standing a couple of yards away from the net. 'By the way, McNamara, that's two-one. And we're winning!' He leered at McNamara, turned, and trotted back downfield.

McNamara nodded stupidly. He couldn't believe it. Couldn't understand it. But it was true! The inept grunts of Larkin's Lot were beating the cool, coordinated skill of McNamara's Death Squad!

McNamara's eyes closed to slits. His face turned to a mask of angry rage. He pointed toward Larkin as if trying to bury the outstretched forefinger in the narrow, weak chest. 'YOU!' he gasped. 'YOU ARE DEAD!' he turned to the rest of his Death Squad team. 'GET 'EM!!!' he screamed at the top of his lungs, and kicked the ball into play.

Gerry Larkin watched the ball sail up into the windswept sea of air. It felt as if everything were in slow motion. He knew that he had all the time in the world. And he felt the power within him waiting, like a great, fiery dragon. He pulled his leg back, feeling the power there. And now his leg was swinging forward, meeting the descending ball as he knew it would. The power coursed from deep within his leg, running down into his foot, into his shoe ... WHAAAAPPPPP!

And the ball rocketed - R O C K E T E D - towards the net, almost taking the heads off the opposing team members. McNamara watching it spin towards him from forty metres out! Forty metres! He stared, knowing that if he were to try to stop it that the force of the ball would kill him ... The ball struck the back of the net, swinging it sharply, swinging until Larkin thought that it would never stop ... The power of it. The glory of it. The crowd started to clap, hesitantly at first, then, more and more powerfully. It was like claps of thunder. 'Larkin, Larkin, Larkin!'

Chapter Nine

That day they beat McNamara's Death Squad nineteen to one. Nineteen to one! And I, Problem Wish Assistant First Class, an Angel who should know better, just stood there and did nothing. Oh! That I could change things now!

Even I have to admit, however, that they did have a good time with their newly found - while decidedly evil - powers. With each game that they played, they lay in the muck of their rotten, devilish deal, soaking up their energies like little piggies at a trough. And who could blame them? Where before they had heard the chants of 'Losers!', now they were heroes of the county! And with each game that they played, they became even more celebrated.

Where before they had lost twenty-seven-nil, now they won. Often by scores that were simply amazing! Larkin's Lot took great joy in devastating the teams that played against them. They took joy in it, but it's sad to say that they lost their humanity along the way, as well as their souls.

While the team had once been losers, at least they had understood the beauty and courage of giving it their best, of trying with their whole heart. But now, of course, with the powers of Lucky Lucy at their disposal, they didn't need to try to win. They just stood on the field and let the power flow through them, controlling them like puppets.

Which, of course they were. Because Lucky Lucy now owned them.

They played ten more teams. And they beat them all. Crowds came from all over the country now, not to laugh at them but to marvel at their skills and abilities. And as for the teams who played and lost to Larkin's Lot? Well, they soon realised that they were doomed to lose from the start. The saddest case I can remember is the young keeper who stood in front of the net, having lost to Larkin's Lot forty-five to nothing. I remember that his name was Brian O'Kane. And he stood in front of that poor net, knowing that he had helplessly let forty-five balls go whizzing past him, and he stood there, crying.

Oh, it was sad. And did Gerry or Fran or Big Jimmy or any of the other Larkin's Lot team members have anything kind to say to the kid who had lost so badly? Not on your life. Instead, they turned their backs, laughing, and walked off the field. Oh, it was a sad, sad day and I'm ashamed to even think about it.

I'm ashamed because, you see, it was partly my fault. I should have done something when I saw them sign the deal with Lucky Lucy. But did I do it? No. I'm afraid I didn't. I let things slide. I let Lucky Lucy get away with murder. I let things go until things couldn't get much worse.

Because, you see, things did get worse. And it started this way ...

'What do you mean they all have measles?' The

tough English accent boomed across the small locker room, almost knocking the assistant coach against the wall. 'They *can't have measles!*'

The small assistant coach gulped audibly. 'I'm afraid they do. I can't do anything about it, you know?' He twisted his green, yellow and white cap into a ball, worried that the Big Man would really lose his temper. 'I mean, I'm not a doctor.'

'Did you talk to the doctor?' the Coach cried.

'Yes, yes, Boss. I talked to the doctor. And you don't have to worry.' The assistant coach grinned, trying to reassure the Big Man. 'They'll all be better ... soon.'

'SOON? HOW SOON!' the Big Man roared.

The assistant coach grovelled on the floor, wishing the ground would open up and swallow him. 'Oh ...' he wavered, '... in about two or three weeks.'

'TWO OR THREE WEEKS! BUT THAT'S IMPOSSIBLE!' The Big Man paced about the room, slapping his giant, capable hands against his side. They had worked too long to get here! Too long! He turned to the quivering assistant coach.

'How many are down with this ... this ... measles?' he asked, his lion-like face red with rage.

'Seven,' his assistant croaked.

'Seven?' The Coach put his hands in his pockets, thinking deeply. 'All right, we'll just have to bring in all of the substitutes and cap a few of the younger lads.'

The assistant coach shook his head. 'No, Boss.' He gulped. 'Seven starters are sick ... and all of the substitutes,' he said miserably.

85

'*All of them?*'

The trembling assistant coach could only nod. He sat down suddenly on the wooden locker-room bench, looking like a lost puppy, waiting for his boss to explode.

'It's too much! Too much!' The Big Man bounded around the floor, looking like a caged lion. 'We've worked hard. The lads have worked hard. And it's paid off! It's finally paid off! The World Cup starts next week. How can we possibly play if we can't field a team?'

And it was true. It was 1998. For two years, the Irish Team had played like they had never played before. Trouncing Spain. Creaming Portugal. Taking on their friends in Northern Ireland and giving them a thrashing. And, the *pièce de résistance* - beating the English team in Wembley Stadium before a packed crowd of sixty thousand fans.

And now, having taken their division by storm, the Irish were favoured to go all the way, to become the holders of the 1998 World Cup. It was within their grasp. After all the hard work ...

... only to have a little thing like measles - *measles* - put it all in the balance.

The Big Man sat suddenly, his head in his hands. He had never felt this bad before. Not after the crazy nil-nil draw which they had received at the hands of Liechtenstein a number of years before. Nor after the arguments with his famous midfielder whom he loved like a son.

Not even after the worst moment of his life - the debacle of the 1995 riot at Lansdowne Road when he'd seen some of his fellow countrymen acting horribly during a match.

No. This was the worst day. The very, very worst. He raised his head, looking at his assistant, feeling the tears welling up behind the usually confident eyes. 'What are we going to do, old son? What the Devil are we going to do?'

The door swung open. A breath of air, blast-furnace hot, sailed through, threatening to roast the Big Man on the spot. And on its tail pranced in a tall, dapper-looking sort dressed in a spotless white suit and tails, and sporting a top hat.

'My dear fellow!' he said, putting out his hand in greeting. 'I'm so sorry for being late! I was down below, you know, celebrating.' He took out a black handkerchief, delicately blotting his sweating forehead. 'Those Salem Witches,' he sighed. 'They'd dance all night, despite being burned at the stake. And the sweat that I work up! It's quite embarrassing!'

The Big Man sat there, staring at this unwelcome intrusion as if the fellow in the white jacket were mad. 'Go away,' he said finally, flicking a finger to the door. 'Out. I don't care what you're selling. Get out and leave me in peace.'

'Ummm,' the dapper fellow said. 'I can understand your impatience.' He shook his head. 'Tut-tut. Measles and all of that. It's such a pity to put the World Cup on the line just because of a miserable little bug.'

The Big Man stared at the visitor in anger. 'How did you know about the measles? I didn't think anybody knew about them.' He turned to his assistant, his eyes flashing. 'Did you tell him about our lads being sick?'

'I haven't seen him before in my life, Boss. Honest!'

Their visitor put a hand up, nodding in agreement. 'That's quite true.' He sniggered slightly. 'At least not in the flesh,' he finished.

'Then how did you find out?' the Coach said, turning to the white-coated visitor. 'How did you know about my problem?'

'Oh, I have my ways,' the visitor stated. 'I know, for instance, that half of your team is ill. Too ill to play football.' He smiled sweetly, pacing now across the small locker-room floor. 'I know that you can't play in the World Cup because you can't field a team. Which is a shame, isn't it, Coach? Because you're favoured to win this year, aren't you?'

The Coach sat miserably on the locker-room bench, each statement from their unwelcome visitor making him cringe with pain. He looked up, staring at the white apparition, feeling suddenly like squeezing the little runt into the size of a football. Suddenly, he had enough. He stood up, towering over their unwelcome guest. 'So what business is it of yours?' he stated, annoyed. 'Now either say something that I don't know, or get out of here.'

The guest gulped. He looked up at the towering figure of the Big Man, and glinted at him with his golden eyes. 'Because,' he stated. 'I can help! My card!' He quickly shoved the gold-embossed card under the Coach's nose, explaining as he did, 'Lucky Lucy, Talent Scout, at your service, Coach. I have seven players who might interest you.'

The Coach looked at him suspiciously. 'Seven?

What teams do they play on?'

Lucky shook his head. 'Teams don't matter, my friend. But let me tell you, these are seven of the best players in the world.'

Now, the Big Man became interested. 'Yeah?' he said, rubbing his jaw. 'How old did you say they were?'

'Oh,' Lucky said carelessly. 'Eleven, twelve. That sort of age.'

'Get out.' The Irish Coach walked toward the door. 'Get out of here before I personally break your neck. You're wasting my time.'

'Now, now,' Lucky Lucy said smoothly. 'They can play football. Great football. There's a striker. Gerry Larkin. He can hit the net from forty, seventy metres out.'

The Big Man shrugged his shoulders. 'So? What's the big deal? Any kid can hit the net. But can he do it at speed?'

Lucy looked at him slyly. 'How's seventy miles an hour grab you?'

The Big Man's jaw dropped open. The assistant coach fell on to the floor. Lucky Lucy smiled brightly. 'It's true! Come see for yourself.'

'You're joking, aren't you, mate?' the Coach said.

Lucky Lucy shook his head. 'Would I lie to you?' he said. 'When you see them, you're not going to believe your eyes. And neither will the world.' Lucky Lucy reached up, patting the Coach on the shoulder. 'You'll see. They'll take you all the way,' he said persuasively. 'You'll win the Cup. And I ...' he muttered out of earshot, 'I'll win their souls for all time.'

Chapter Ten

'I don't believe it!' Gerry Larkin whispered reverently. 'We're here! We're playing! We're actually professional football players!' They stood on the grass of the huge football pitch, gawking at the international football arena in Paris, France, not believing that they were actually there. The stands were empty, the field silent. The green grass of the pitch seemed to stretch on forever, like a great, green magic carpet. And tomorrow they would play. They would actually play international football against some of the best, the brightest, the most talented teams in the world.

They would play in the 1998 World Cup. It was a moment that he would never forget, no matter what happened. Gerry Larkin couldn't believe it, and he said so again. 'I don't believe it,' he gasped.

Fran Clifford turned to him, smiling savagely. 'I told you, didn't I?' she said confidently. 'I told you. If you want something bad enough, if you give it your all, you can make it happen. There's no such thing as 'I can't',' she finished.

Gerry Larkin glanced at her. 'Having Lucky Lucy around kind of helped, though,' he said with a worried voice.

Fran sniffed. 'Maybe.' She eyed her friend coolly. 'What's the matter? Don't you like winning? Don't you like being picked by one of the best coaches in the world to play in the World Cup?'

'I guess so,' Gerry said slowly, his large Adam's apple working. Yeah, he liked winning, he thought. But at the price of their souls? That price seemed outrageously high. But the other members of the team didn't look at it that way.

The past six months had floated by like a dream, their individual talents and skills increasing as time went by. For the first few weeks, Lucky Lucy hadn't been involved at all. He was nowhere to be seen. Then one day, he appeared suddenly, just as they were beginning another practice session.

'Hello!' he said, waving a white-gloved hand. 'Just thought I'd come along to protect my investment.'

Fran walked up to him. 'What are you doing here?' she said suspiciously, hands on hips.

'I'm your manager, remember?' he said. 'You did sign the contract.' He put up a hand. The parchment contract appeared suddenly accompanied by a small flash of lightning and the sickening smell of sulphur.

Fran rolled her eyes. 'You can stop the fireworks displays, Lucky,' she said. 'We get the idea.'

'Sorry.' He held the contract out toward her for a quick inspection, then pulled it back before she really had a chance to read it properly. 'See?' he said smoothly. 'It's in the small print. I'm your manager as well as your agent.' He rolled the contract up again, giving it back to the air. It disappeared in a puff of smoke. 'I organise matches, training sessions, royalties and fees. You name it, I do it.' He smiled at her. 'You all signed the contract, didn't you? Which means,' he said with glee, 'that I own you.'

She nodded sceptically, putting up a hand. 'For six months, remember. You own us for just six months.'

Lucky nodded. 'That's right. For six months. And at the end of that period, well ...' He gazed at her small figure. 'I'm sure you'll grow to love winning, won't you, Frances? And then, it's just a matter of signing a life-time contract, isn't it?'

Frances Clifford gazed at him. 'We'll see about that. You just make sure that we keep winning,' she said.

Lucky Lucy nodded. 'Oh, don't you worry about that. I have that all taken care of.' He smiled that dapper, silk-smooth smile of his, and left her.

Lucky had stuck to his end of the bargain, of course. He organised a whole series of matches. First, they took on and squashed every school that had the unfortunate experience to play against them. Then, Lucky organised some matches with older teams. Four weeks ago, for instance, Larkin's Lot had played against Cork. The Cork team coach had at first turned down the idea of playing against a group of kids, but Lucky had annoyed him.

'What's the matter, coach?' Lucky said. 'Afraid of a group of kids?'

That did it. The Cork coach had smiled grimly. 'Okay, Mr Lucy,' he said. 'But tell that team of yours that we aren't going to hold back simply because they're a bunch of youngsters.'

'Oh, I don't think you'll have to worry about that,' Lucky had said, smiling. Which he didn't. The Cork team was thrashed thirty-six to one. The Cork coach went home thinking that he'd never get over the humiliation of their defeat. 'I don't believe it,' he said. 'Who are those guys?' He had never seen so much talent in a bunch of kids. And he couldn't get over that striker. Larkin, wasn't it? He was amazing. The Cork players were afraid of him. When Larkin kicked the ball, it moved with such speed - such force - that it could tear an opposing player's head off.

Larkin was dangerous. The Cork coach could only shake his head in amazement.

And then had come the moment - only a few days ago - when Lucky had turned up and had announced to the team, 'Do I have a surprise for you!'

And there, standing beside their team manager, was a man whom each of the seven Larkin's Lot players recognised instantly. A man whom they thought of as a saint. It was *him*, they all gasped. The Big Man!

The Irish manager surveyed the group of seven with a look somewhere between amusement and disbelief. 'Alright, laddies - oh, and you too, young lady,' he nodded toward Fran, 'show me what you've got.'

And they did. They showed him. And Big Jack had never seen anything like it. A huge smile appeared on his face. And he knew that they could win!

And now, a couple of days later, here they were. In France. Playing in the biggest, the most famous series of matches ever. The World Cup!

Standing in the grounds of the huge echoing football stadium, Gerry Larkin shook his head. 'It's amazing, Fran,' he said. 'But at the price of our souls? I don't know.'

'Oh, stop your mouthing,' she said. Then she held up a newspaper. It was the morning edition of the *Irish Times*. The banner headline read: IRISH KIDS TAKE ON THE WORLD!

'See?' Fran snickered arrogantly, 'we're famous! And it's all down to Lucky. Not bad for a couple of souls.'

Gerry shook his head sadly. 'That contract is only going to get us into more hot water than we bargained for.'

'Stop worrying about the contract!' Fran answered brusquely. 'Besides, the contract is up in a couple of days. We can talk about our souls then. In the meantime, let's win!'

But Gerry Larkin now wasn't sure that winning was all that important.

Chapter Eleven

Lucky was on his mobile phone, talking urgently. 'Look, Adolf,' he said, threateningly, 'you worry about your business and I'll worry about mine. The Larkin's Lot contract is up in a couple of days.' He listened, grinning. 'Oh, they'll sign the other contract, The Eternal Souls Contract, that's for certain. I know they will. They like winning too much! And when they do, I have them for ever!' He giggled slyly, the gold eyes glinting. 'Now you just make sure that temperature is up! When Larkin's Lot sign their souls away, I'm going to treat all seven of them to a visit to our establishment. And I want things hot down there. *Hot!* Do you understand me?'

'Excuse me, Lucky?' Lucky Lucy turned suddenly. The Irish assistant coach was standing there impatiently. 'The Boss wants your people out on the field. Right now.'

Lucky nodded. 'Gotta go, Adolf. But turn the heat up. And no snivelling this time!' He turned to the assistant. 'So, let's get them on the field,' he said.

It was an amazing day. The seven team members, now dressed in green, orange and white, walked slowly out of the tunnel into the noonday sun. Around them, a hundred thousand people burst into cheers. The seven of them stood back a little, awed by the power of it all. Fran, Big Jimmy, the Bright Brothers, Tommy Reynolds, Harold Smyth and Gerry Larkin - all of them stood there for a minute, trying to get their bearings.

'Go on!' the assistant coach yelled at them. 'Get out there!'

Fran gulped, waving a hand. 'We're going!' she said, and turned to the rest of the team. They all looked nervous. 'Come on, you guys. This is just like any other match.'

'You sure?' Big Jimmy said. He nodded across the pitch where the other team was now entering the stadium. 'That's Italy over there. You know?' He gulped, the fat of his face swishing around. 'They play tough.'

'Yeah,' Harold said, whimpering with fear. 'What happens if they beat us?'

Fran shook her head. 'They aren't going to beat us. Not with Lucky Lucy behind us.' She looked up the sideline. The other four Irish players were there, waiting for them. 'Come on, let's go.'

The older, experienced Irish team members couldn't believe that they were playing with kids. Andy, as team captain, had said as much. 'Ah, Coach?' He had swallowed hard, trying to get up the courage. 'Look, I know that we're in trouble, but playing with kids?'

The Big Man had eyed him, somewhat annoyed. 'I know it's unusual. I had to fight with FIFA to get them to go along with this. Besides,' he'd said evenly, 'what choice do we have? We either play with the kids or we forfeit the matches. So what's it

96

to be?' He looked the captain in the eye.

The Ireland team captain had looked glum. 'The other lads aren't going to like it.'

'They're going to have to like it. Besides, wait 'til you see these kids play. None of you is going to believe it.' Andy had shaken his head. He didn't believe it. He didn't believe that a group of kids from sixth class were playing with the Irish squad! And a girl, for God's sake! But that's the way it was.

Now, standing there, he watched as the group of seven weak-looking little kids walked up to them, their green and white jerseys flopping around them like beach towels. 'Hiya,' the girl said weakly. She held up a hand in embarrassed greeting. Andy sighed.

'You're playing keeper, aren't you?' he asked. Fran nodded. 'OK, well make sure you watch your corners.' He looked at the rest of them. 'You all know what positions you're playing?'

The rest of Larkin's Lot nodded, almost intelligently. Andy glanced at the other three adult team members. Phil, Paul and John could only shake their heads in frustration. 'What a way to run a squad,' Phil said. 'I just hope the Big Man knows what he's doing.'

'Right.' Andy looked at his team and sighed. 'Try not to mess up too much, will you, kids?' he asked. Then they ran out on to the pitch.

'I've got it!' Big Jimmy screamed. It was ten minutes into the match. The score was still nil-all, and the Irish were only now finding their feet. The Italians couldn't believe that they were playing against kids.

97

The crowd couldn't believe that the Irish were playing kids. For the first few minutes, all that the Italian side could do was laugh. But Fran Clifford, standing in goal, knew that this was going to change. And soon.

Now, Big Jimmy ran down the pitch like a lumbering elephant. The Italian in front of him looked up, seeing the humongous tub of fat sloshing down toward him, and realised that he was going to get squashed as flat as his mother's pizza. '*Mamma mia!*' he screamed in a high-pitched voice. Big Jimmy never saw him. The ball was floating down from the heavens, down from the seventy-metre WHACK that Fran had given it.

It clobbered Big Jimmy right between the eyes, careening off his forehead at tremendous speed, smacking the astonished Italian right in the nose.

The Italian's face went blank, and he collapsed like a cardboard cut-out. 'Next time keep out of my way, pizza face,' Big Jimmy screamed at him. The Italian couldn't hear him because the Italian had been knocked unconscious.

The ball, meanwhile, went skittering back to Andy, who couldn't believe what he had just seen. In over twenty years of playing the game, he had never seen anyone knocked unconscious by a football. Andy stood there in shock.

'Gangway!' He turned. Behind him, three Italians were converging on him rapidly. But running straight up the field was Tommy Reynolds, his thick glasses looking like a pair of headlights. 'Give it to me, Andy!'

Andy nodded, somewhat stupefied at Tommy's

tremendous speed, and kicked it back to him. The Italians saw the ball coming toward them and never had a chance. As the three Italians swooped toward the ball, Tommy Reynolds dropped to his stomach, sliding down the field like he was on a toboggan, taking the ball right out from under them.

The Italians, meanwhile, looking incredulously at Tommy Reynolds, didn't think to keep out of each other's way. They crashed together, coming to rest like a motorway pile-up.

Tommy flicked the ball toward Gerry Larkin. Gerry took the ball neatly and moved down the right sideline. He looked behind him. The Italian defence had crumbled. Larkin stopped. The keeper stood in his box, waiting, grinning at the young boy who could not possibly do anything with the ball.

Gerry grinned back. He wound back his leg, feeling the energy move through it suddenly, kicking the ball like an automaton.

The ball came directly at the Italian keeper. He stood there, his jaw dropping, amazed and horrified at the speed. The ball hit him smack in the belly, driving him back toward the net.

The keeper collapsed, and as he hit the dirt, he released the ball ... which rolled gently past the goal line. And the five thousand Irish fans sitting in the stands went wild! It was one-nil, Ireland.

'This is kind of fun,' Gerry said to Andy as he ran back into position. The Irish team captain could only nod, his mouth hanging open in astonishment at the tremendous force of the score. 'Ah ... good goal, kid.'

Gerry waved at him. 'Thanks!' The ball was put

promptly back into play.

It was Fran's turn to shine next. The Italians, still reeling from the shock of the last goal, were trying to equalise quickly. Fran, standing just outside the box, saw the ball being dribbled neatly into the open space in midfield. 'Almost!' she pointed to the Bright Brother. 'Grab that guy!' Almost nodded, running forward. But as he did, the ball was passed expertly between his legs, passed to the Italian forward who was dashing up midfield.

Fran saw him and back-pedalled. She was out of position and she knew it. She looked quickly behind her. She had made a huge mistake, she realised suddenly. The entire right-hand side of the goal was gaping open.

The Italian saw her predicament and pounced. The ball drove viciously toward the net. Fran, having no other option, jumped to the right, both arms outstretched, her entire small little body now horizontal to the ground. The fingers reaching into space ... just making contact with the streaking ball, pushing it beyond the right-hand corner with just inches to spare.

It was a defensive move of a lifetime, and the crowd knew it. They roared her name with approval. 'FRANCES! FRANCES! FRANCES!'

She turned to them, waving, glancing back upfield at Paul, the great midfielder who looked at her as if she were a ghost. 'Kind of fun, isn't it, Paul?' she said. He could only nod.

The Italian team never had a chance. In the heat of the French afternoon, they were beaten solidly, four-nil. And at the end of the match, the pride of

Italy walked off the field, their heads slumped in the despair of defeat.

As they walked off, Big Jimmy waved at them. 'Too bad, lads,' he called. 'Better luck next year!' They didn't look back at him. 'Losers!' he said to Fran, shaking his head. 'It must be horrible to be a loser!'

Fran grinned. 'I wonder what it's going to be like to win the World Cup?' she said confidently. And they both broke into laughter, the rest of Larkin's Lot joining them.

Gerry Larkin, walking behind, heard the exchange. He shook his head sadly. He remembered what it was like to be a loser. And he looked at the Italian team, walking with the sting of defeat in their stomachs, and felt sorry for them.

Chapter Twelve

'This is it! This is the Big One!' The Big Man himself stood in front of the eleven players, grinning broadly. 'You've all played like I've never seen a team play before. Especially you seven. You players from Larkin's Lot.' He turned to them. 'A special thanks to the younger members of the squad.'

Gerry Larkin glanced around the Visitors' locker room at the other members of the team. His six friends were smiling like movie stars. In fact, they were behaving like movie stars, which didn't sit too well with Gerry Larkin.

Since that first match, they had been plagued by hundreds of fans, all wanting their autographs. The media had turned their hotel into a circus, always wanting interviews. Occasionally, Lucky Lucy would prance out of the plush elevator, a couple of the team members in tow. He would stand in front of the bright lights of the camera and the forest of microphones, polishing his nails. 'Five minutes,' he would say. 'Make the interview snappy!' And the group of international press would barrage the Larkin's Lot team members with a million questions.

With all the attention, and with their winning ways, Larkin's Lot had changed, Gerry knew. And he didn't like it. Not one bit. The team - Tommy, Big

Jimmy, Harold, the Bright Brothers and especially Fran - seemed now like a particularly nasty family of royalty. They kept themselves apart from the rest of the Irish team. They had their dinners alone. They talked only of winning. They didn't even appreciate that they were lucky to be in the World Cup at all! Gerry thought.

And he knew that in many ways he had become just as cold, just as arrogant, just as snooty, as the rest of his so-called friends. And Gerry didn't like the changes that were happening to him. Not at all.

The past two weeks had flown. Since the first match with Italy, they had mown down the rest of the teams in their path like a hacksaw through peanut butter. It had been so easy! The Dutch had been clobbered by Ireland, six to two. They never knew what hit them.

England had been the worst match. Larkin's Lot had blown away the English side, twelve-nil. As they played, and as the talented English squad wilted before the devilish onslaught of the Irish performance, Larkin's Lot team members started to laugh at them. Making cat-calls. 'Loser!' Tommy Reynolds had hissed at the star English midfielder. 'Losers!' the Bright Brothers had screamed at the dumbfounded English forwards. 'Go back home!' Fran had screamed wickedly at the defeated, humiliated English captain.

But the worst part of it all was the fact that Larkin's Lot wouldn't even let the older - and more experienced - Ireland team members play now. They kept the ball away from them, playing as if they were their own team of seven. Paul, Andy,

John and Phil never had a chance with the ball. Effectively, they were kept out of the match. For the older members, who had been a part of the Irish team for so many years, it was a humiliating experience.

Watching the sad looks on the faces of the older players, Gerry Larkin remembered when he had tried to play on the McNamara team, and what it had been like to be kept away from the ball. Sitting in the locker room, thinking about it, he lowered his head in disgust. He was disgusted because he knew that he was as bad as his friends, that he treated the older players with contempt, which wasn't right. But it seemed too late to do anything about it now.

And now they were in the World Cup Final. Unbelievable as it seemed to Gerry Larkin, they had made it almost all the way. Only a single match separated them from the hallowed trophy! Only one more! And for four days, now, the forthcoming match was all that the Larkin's Lot players had talked about. And they waited, confidently, for the great day to come, telling the press on the second day before the match that they were going to play inspired football. Bragging to the press on the day before the match that the opposing French side would be swept away like so many misfits.

And now, five minutes before the match, they sat in the locker room, only half-listening as the Great Irish Coach told them once more how proud he was of them. And they ignored his praises because they thought that they were greater than anything he might have to say.

'Larkin! You all right?' Gerry looked up. The

Coach was standing over him, a joyous grin on his long, intelligent face.

Gerry nodded dumbly. 'Yes, sir,' he said, knowing that he wasn't.

'Good. Because now, we're going to go out there and win the World Cup!' Gerry nodded again. He looked at the arrogant faces of his team-mates, and felt sick.

The eleven of them stood, and started toward the door. Gerry saw Fran, grabbing her by the elbow. 'Can I talk to you?' he said suddenly.

She looked at him. 'Do you have to right now?' She grinned. 'We have a match to win, you know.'

He nodded. 'Yeah, I know.' He sat, looking at his shoes. 'Look, I don't know about this any more.'

'Know about what?'

'You know,' Gerry said slowly. 'All this winning. It's all a lie.'

Fran glared at him. 'Get with it, Larkin. How is it a lie?' She stood over him, her small figure seeming about to pounce. 'You signed the contract, just like the rest of us. You knew what you were getting into.'

He nodded. 'But it's not right, don't you see that?' He stood, pacing around the floor. 'This isn't our talent. It's Lucky Lucy's - the Devil's!' he cried suddenly. 'It's the Devil's power, not ours.'

'So what's the big deal?' Fran stated coldly. 'We gave our souls up for a few months, and look where it's gotten us.' She leaned forward toward him, hissing at him. 'We're in the World Cup, Larkin! Did you ever think you'd be in the World Cup?'

He shook his head. 'But it doesn't matter because

we didn't get here by ourselves. Besides, we've all changed.'

'How have we changed?' Fran said angrily. 'Says who?'

'Says me!' He stood up, his long, gangling frame filling the locker room. 'You used to be a good friend, Fran. Now you're ...' he stopped, looking for the words. 'Cold. Unfriendly. Arrogant.'

'Oh yeah?' she said icily. 'Well, let me tell you something, Gerry Larkin. I think you're angry because you were always a loser. You stank before Lucky Lucy came along. And now that you're becoming a winner, you can't handle it! You just can't handle winning!' She spun away from him, and left the room.

As she left, Lucky Lucy came blowing in on a gust of hot air. In his hand, he held a bright red piece of paper. With a flourish, he presented it to Gerry. 'You might as well sign now,' he said gleefully. 'Everyone else has.'

Gerry's brain was still ringing with Fran's last fiery retort. He looked at Lucy. 'Sign what?' he said dully.

'Why, the new contract, of course! The Eternal Soul's Contract.' Lucy looked at his diamond-studded watch. 'Your six-month probationary period runs out in one hour. You have to sign now, or you go back to your old self.' Lucy smiled at him sweetly. 'And you wouldn't like that, would you, Gerry?'

'You certain that it's time?' Gerry asked.

Lucky nodded. 'Oh, yes. I'm sure of it. In sixty minutes, it will be exactly six months from when

106

you signed the original deal. It was your idea, remember? You wanted a six-months out clause.'

'And if I don't sign?'

'I think you'll sign, Gerry,' Lucky Lucy said. 'After all, you're in the final of the World Cup, aren't you? Your team, your family, your country, the whole world will be looking at you.' Lucky grinned, the light glinting from his white teeth. 'And I don't think you'll want to lose. Not now.' Lucky held out a pen, waiting expectantly. 'Come on. Everyone else on the team has signed. You might as well get it out of the way, too,' Lucky stated with a bored expression.

'I don't know now,' Gerry said angrily. 'I don't care whether my so-called team-mates have signed or not.' He looked at Lucky, and saw evil lurking behind that soft, smooth face. Still, he couldn't let down his team, could he? 'Talk to me in an hour,' he said. And with that, Gerry Larkin ran out the door and on to the field.

Chapter Thirteen

When I saw that six of Larkin's Lot had signed the contract, I panicked! Of course, I should have come down to good old Earth months earlier to deal with Lucky Lucy personally, but up until that point I thought that the team would realise just what Lucky was all about. 'You just wait, Michael,' I said to my most favourite of Archangels, 'They'll play along for six months, then they'll get smart. And Lucky will lose again!' I laughed.

Michael, polishing his trumpet, only stared at me. 'You want to bet? They get a taste of winning, and they'll want to stay with Lucky forever. If I were you,' he stated, arching that eyebrow of his up into a rainbow of light, 'I'd get those wings of yours in gear and get right down there. They need some help.'

But would I listen? No way. I just sat up there on my cloud, watching the world go by, and thought the problem would solve itself.

But then, I watched on as Lucky brought the contract to the six of them. I watched as they all grinned with happiness, signing without a second thought. 'THEY DON'T KNOW WHAT THEY'RE DOING!' I shouted.

Michael glanced up and looked at me smugly. 'I told you so,' he said.

'Gerry hasn't signed! I still have a chance!'

'True,' Michael nodded. 'But if he signs, they're dead meat. Lucky will own their souls forever.' He looked at me. 'I'd get moving, my friend. You don't have much time.'

'Right! Right!' I turned to him. 'I'm off!'

'Good hunting,' Michael said. And I started flapping my wings to beat the Devil, gliding down between the great clouds of wishes shooting up into the sky, wishing for a moment that I was still only an Apprentice Wish Angel, and that I didn't have to confront Lucky Lucy once again, because that always meant trouble. And this time would be no exception ...

'And that's the end of the first half! Ireland is leading in this, the 1998 World Cup Final, by a score of two to one. It has been a remarkably close score considering the exceptional talent of the Irish squad. But today, they just don't seem to be in top form, leaving the Frenchmen a fighting chance ...'

'Turn off that radio!' Fran Clifford shouted at Tommy as she stalked into the locker room. 'What a miserable first half! Only two-one. What's wrong with us?'

She turned to Gerry Larkin. 'What's wrong with you, Larkin? You had at least four great scoring opportunities. What happened to them?'

'I don't know,' Gerry said, shaking his head forlornly. And he didn't. His powerful hotfoot simply didn't seem to be working.

Lucky Lucy, who had followed them into the locker room, grinned slyly. 'Perhaps I can put some

... heat ... on the subject,' he said.

Fran turned to him. 'Well?' she said threateningly.

Lucky turned and walked toward Gerry. 'As you know,' he said, 'today is the day that your contract runs out.' He glanced at his watch. 'In fact, it runs out in exactly five minutes.'

'So what? Everyone has already signed the new agreement. This Eternal Souls Contract you gave to us. So what's the contract got to do with it?' Fran asked, annoyed.

Lucky shook his head, his face now only six inches from Gerry Larkin's nose. 'Not everyone has signed it, I'm afraid,' Lucky said. The six other members of Larkin's Lot turned to Gerry. 'Gerard hasn't signed it. And I thought I'd give him a taste of what not signing would mean.' Lucky smiled maliciously. 'I took away some of your power. I suspect you felt rather awkward out on the field, didn't you, Gerard?'

'You haven't signed it?' Fran breathed. '*You haven't signed it!* What's wrong with you, Larkin? Sign it! Sign it right now! We need that hotfoot of yours!'

The other members of the team crowded toward him, forcing him back toward the wall. Gerry felt as if he was going to get pummelled. To one side were the Bright Brothers, making threatening noises. To the other was Big Jimmy, his arms crossed, his tonne of fat rubbing uncomfortably against Gerry's side. Lucky produced the new contract and a pen, thrusting it under Gerry's nose.

'Sign it!' Fran growled. Gerry looked at them, and realised suddenly that it was time to take a stand.

'No,' he whispered. 'I won't sign.'

'What!' Fran gasped. 'If you don't sign, the whole contract goes up in flames. We *all* have to sign, isn't that right, Lucky?'

Lucky looked like a tiger cornering its prey. 'That's right, Frances. You all have to sign. Otherwise, CRRIIICCKKKK!' he made a gagging noise, drawing his manicured finger along his throat, 'Your powers are gone. The French team will come back. And ... you'll lose! In front of a worldwide audience of millions, you'll become the miserable, untalented, inept players that you actually are!' He grinned. 'And I don't think that any of you want that. Do you?'

Fran leaned toward Gerry menacingly. 'Sign! Sign now!'

'Or what?' Gerry yelled back.

'Or this!' she shouted. 'Big Jimmy! Grab him!' Big Jimmy grabbed Gerry's hands. Big Jimmy's strength had always been amazing, but with Lucky Lucy behind him, Gerry had no chance. Slowly, Big Jimmy opened Gerry's hand. Lucky thrust the pen into it. Now, they dragged the struggling, shaking paw of Gerry Larkin toward the contract. Closer. The pen was now only an inch from the glittering red and gold contract.

Gerry closed his eyes, fighting with all his strength. He was losing! In a moment, he would be forced to sign. And his soul - and the souls of his friends - would be lost forever to the scheming evil that was Lucky Lucy ...

... and then the door banged open. A cold wind blew into the locker room. A flash of light, the toll of a hundred bells, and in I flew ...

'Gerry! Run!' He looked up at me, astonished. 'Run! Right now!' I pelted across the small space of the locker room, grabbing the throat of Lucky Lucy in a death grip.

'You!' he shrieked. 'Get off me. By Hades, if you even touch me ...'

'Now, now,' I said. 'No swearing. Not in front of the children.'

'*Get off!*' He grabbed me by the wings, flinging me across the room into the metal lockers like a sack of gilded feathers. As I hit, the metal doors flew open.

Lucky Lucy looked at me, his eyes a horrible glinting gold. He looked down. The contract was no longer in his hand. In fact, I had it.

'Is this what you're looking for?' I asked, waving it at him.

'You're going to make me lose my temper!' he shouted. His voice was no longer all sweetness and light. It sounded like a great foghorn, reverberating around the small room.

'Good,' I sniffed. 'Maybe it will remind the children just what kind of a monster you are.'

Lucky Lucy stood there, huffing and puffing. 'Give me my contract!' he screamed.

'All right. Take it,' I said nicely. Then, I held it up and tore it in two ...

'Aaarrgghh!' He looked at me, his face now red with rage. 'YOU! YOU'RE ALWAYS IN THE WAY. NOW YOU'LL PAY FOR THIS!'

'Will I?' I said, nonchalantly. 'Well, come and get me.'

I watched, knowing what would happen now. It

doesn't take much to make Lucky Lucy fly off the handle. His face grew redder and redder. The cheeks distorted, seeming to break through the soft pink skin. Bulges appeared on his forehead, growing as I watched. Larger and larger, they grew and then the horns broke through the skin, small droplets of blood dripping down his face.

His body grew, splitting the clothes from his back. Beneath the ripped fabric, I could see the scales of his lizard-like body. The great ribbed wings unfolded behind him, seeming to fill the room. And as he transformed before their eyes, Larkin's Lot backed off, cowering into a corner.

'I'M COMING TO GET YOU!' it roared.

'Come ahead,' I said modestly. 'No one's stopping you.'

It launched itself toward me on the destructive wings of its evilness... and all I had to do was step out of the way. Lucky saw me move and tried to stop. But its anger and ugliness had prompted it to throw itself at me without thinking. It plummeted toward me like a falling brick, unable to stop itself.

Lucy hit the back of the open locker with a satisfying THUMP!

'Come here!' I ordered the team members. 'Help me to close this!'

I guess Lucky's sudden transformation had really scared them. They didn't think to disobey me Instead, they helped me to shove the locker door closed. There was some banging, of course, and a lot of swearing. It took all of our combined strength to get it closed, but, at last, it shut with a satisfying 'click'. I turned, smiling at them. 'There. We've done

113

it! We've caged the Devil!'

'Did you see that thing?' Fran said, rubbing her eyes. 'I forgot how ugly it was.'

I smiled at her. 'And except for Gerry, you would have signed that contract to give all of your souls to that thing forever.' I smiled as gently as I could. 'Do you think it would ever be worth it, Fran?'

She shook her head. 'No,' she said. 'Not for anything.' She looked at her team-mates. 'We were pretty stupid, weren't we?' she said to them. They all nodded in agreement. Then she stared at me, and her eyes opened wide, as if she saw me for the first time.

'But who are you?' she gasped. 'Look at you!'

I'll admit, I was something of a sight. Thank goodness I had worn my old gown rather than the new one. It was always the same when I met Lucky. And now, it was torn in a dozen places. And as for my wings? Gold tarnishes quickly in the presence of any devil. And when Lucky Lucy is around, well, they look as brown as old bronze.

I smiled at her. 'I'll explain all that later.'

Beneath me, there was a sudden pounding on the door. 'LET ME OUT OF HERE!' it roared. 'RIGHT NOW! YOU LET ME OUT OF HERE OR I'M GOING TO TEAR YOUR WINGS OFF!'

There was a knock on the dressing room door. Jack poked his head in. 'Five minutes, laddies,' he said. 'You best get out on the field. And play a little better in the second half, will you?' He grinned. 'You're scaring me a little.' He glanced at me. 'Who's your friend?' he asked, looking at me.

I looked back at him blankly. 'I ... ah ...'

'He's a new recruit to Larkin's Lot,' Fran said thinking quickly. 'He plays defence.'

'Well, if he's as good as you lot, we might let him try-out for next season. Now get on out there and play.'

Larkin's Lot nodded as one person. The door closed, and we all stood there for a moment, me trying to keep the locker door closed on Lucky, the rest trying to figure out what to do next.

It was Fran who realised. 'Our powers,' she remembered. 'What time is it?' she cried.

Harold Smyth looked at his watch. 'Only another thirty seconds!' he said. 'Thirty more seconds until we're nothing again!'

'I heard that!' Lucky's giggling voice came through the locker door. 'So now, children, what will you do ...? HA HA! ... you'll be the laughing stocks of the world!'

'Not true, Lucky,' I said. 'They can play their best. That's all they have to do.'

I heard him muttering. I turned to the team. 'You go out there and play. Don't worry about losing. Play your very best. But remember, don't believe in the powers that Lucky gave you. Believe in yourselves! That's the biggest power that you could ever wish for. A belief in your own self.' I smiled at them.

'What about you?' Gerry asked.

I grinned. 'I think I'll stay here for a bit. Lucky and I have some catching up to do, don't we, Lucky?' I said to the locker door.

'DROP DEAD!' it screamed.

'Temper, temper,' I warned. I glanced at the team,

so relieved that I had been in time. 'Go on, I urged them. 'Go play football.'

Harold Smyth looked at his watch again. 'It's time,' he said sadly.

There was a sputtering noise. Then a sound like a billion dogs baying loudly. A clap of thunder and a shower of light. And I watched as I saw them become once more the Larkin's Lot that they had been. I looked as their arrogance and pride and anger fell from them like a dirty blanket. Now, they were just kids again. Kids who wanted to play football.

They looked at each other, and I saw the fear in their eyes.

'We're going to lose,' Fran said.

I shook my head. 'Not if you play your best,' I said.

Gerry Larkin turned, studying the faces of his friends. They looked normal, he thought. No longer arrogant. No longer angry. They were simply the kids from Larkin's Lot. And no matter what happened now, they would be winners.

'We don't have to lose,' he said, his mouth creeping into a grin. 'We don't have to lose because I have a plan.'

Despite myself, I listened. And as I did, I smiled, thinking that this just might work.

Chapter Fourteen

' ... and it's ten minutes to go. Ireland two, France two. And oh, what a match!' the announcer said. Gerry knelt on the sideline, trying to get his breath. He heard the screaming from the dugout. He turned his head and watched the Big Man jump up and down.

'What's wrong with you kids? You're throwing it all away!' Jack shouted. Gerry could only shake his head in amusement. Jack was right, of course. They had thrown it all away. When they had refused to sign Lucky's contract, they had thrown away greatness to become ordinary kids again. But Gerry was glad. Now, Larkin looked back into the field, trying to see if his plan was still holding together.

Gerry was getting worried. For the first thirty-five minutes of the second half, they had let the experienced Irish team players have the ball. Larkin's Lot had held back, all of them except Fran playing around midfield.

The French, suspecting that the Irish had another amazingly adept play up their sleeves, hung back, waiting, afraid that if they committed themselves, they would be swarmed upon by the anger and might of the Irish.

The French, however, had put together an equalising score. Fran had watched, frightened, as the ball blasted into the net. Still, the opposing team held back, waiting for the Irish to turn on their magic once again ...

The Irish team captain was confused. For almost two weeks, now, the elder players had seen little of the ball. He didn't understand why the Larkin's Lot players were suddenly so adamant that Paul, Phil, John and Andy should find themselves in possession of the small round object which was the subject of so much attention. But they were pleased. Until they realised that the Larkin's Lot players seemed unwilling to get into the action.

'Hey, Larkin!' Andy screamed. 'Get over here! Come on, this is the final!' Gerry looked downfield. It was a line-out. He had to get back into position. Anxiously, he stood up, his long frame feeling again like a giraffe's. Awkwardly, he started trotting downfield, hoping that his feet would keep him upright for another few minutes. He looked at the clock. Five more minutes. The score was tied. That was as bad as a loss, he knew. If they had a penalty shoot-out, Fran would get creamed.

And they would lose.

The French threw the ball in. They tore upfield toward a cowering Harold Smyth. Harold saw them charging toward them, screamed, turned and ran. As the French midfielder watched the Irish team cower in front of the French attack, a grin broke out on his face. Savagely, he screamed at his team-mates, and they all broke toward the Irish goal.

They knew! Gerry realised suddenly. They knew that something was wrong. And now it was going to fall apart. The ruse that Ireland was holding back to finish the French off was blown. They'd have to do something!

As the ball came upfield, he heard screaming. The Great Irish Coach looked like he was going to have a coronary. The usually calm face of the Big Man was a mottled red. Gerry turned back upfield, spotting Big Jimmy. 'Get him!' Gerry yelled, pointing to the charging French player.

Jimmy nodded dumbly. He started moving downfield. Even though he did not have the immense powers that he once had, Big Jimmy was still a pretty impressive sight. The fat sloshed, right-left, right-left, as he pounded toward the skinny Frenchman.

The poor French midfielder thought that Big Jimmy was going to kill him. He gave a yelp of fear, and flicked the ball sideways ... right into the path of the German referee who had moved over to get a better look. Big Jimmy, following the ball to the best of his morose capability, looked up long enough to see the black-clad referee start to blow his whistle as if trying to stop an on-coming freight train. Big Jimmy hit the brakes, but it was useless. The ref found himself squashed under a tonne of Irish lard.

'Get off!' he screamed in his German accent. '*Gotterzimmer-minder!* Get off me!' Big Jimmy, sitting on the grass of the international French stadium, looked around dumbly, wondering where the ref had gone to.

The ball meantime had squirted downfield. Gerry, way out of position, looked to see where the other players were. He sighed with relief when he saw Paul and Phil move into their defensive positions. Neither of these great Irish team-mates had any intention of letting the ball get past them ... until the Bright Brothers made their appearance.

Almost and Not Quite had seen the referee get impaled by Big Jimmy, and had watched as the ball skittered downfield. Now, knowing that they hadn't done anything to help in the second half, they decided to make up for it. They charged forward, the pair of redheads coming in toward the ball from opposite sides of the field like small red rockets. Babb and McGrath looked up just in time to save their own hides. They screamed at the charging Bright twins, who swerved suddenly. McGrath, trying to get out of the way, ran toward Babb who was also trying to get out of the way ...

... the ball, meanwhile, had been picked up by the French forward, who was studying the professional Irish defensive backs closely, looking for an opportunity. He didn't see the Bright Brothers at first, but was justly amazed when the two clobbered their own defensive contingent. Now, four Irish jerseys lay on the ground, struggling like a group of angry snakes.

He heard a scream. He looked across at the Irish dug-out. The Irish manager had fainted and was being carried off the field.

Now, the French forward looked up. Between himself and the Irish goal was only one Irish defender and the Irish keeper. He looked at the clock. Sixty seconds! It was his chance.

He moved forward quickly, getting ready to let loose with one of his patented, deadly strikes ...

... which is exactly when Lucky Lucy forced its way out of the locker. 'GET OFF,' it hissed. Its strength was incredible! It opened the door with such force that I hit the opposite wall like a ping-pong ball.

'Lucy! Get back in here!' I ordered.

It only grinned at me. 'Not for a billion souls,' it said to me evilly. 'Now, I have to settle a little score with some friends of yours.' It moved, then, flying swiftly out of the room.

I got my wings working, and followed it ...

... the Frenchman looked up. What he saw made him stop in his tracks. He screamed. Above him, Lucky waved a little. 'Hello, and how are we today?' it said. Then, it streaked down toward the field.

Gerry saw Lucky and the ball at the same time. The Frenchman had let the ball roll forward, toward him. Fran came out of the box, charging toward the loose ball. 'Get back up forward!' she ordered, gasping. He nodded. 'Look out for Lucy!' Gerry shouted.

'Don't you worry about Lucy. You just play football!' I had made my way out of the locker room on my set of bent-up wings, and was doing my best to keep Lucy away from the Larkin's Lot players. I knew what he was after. Lucy might not be able to take their souls, now. But he could cause them immense damage. As I watched, I saw him plunge toward Tommy Reynolds. Reynolds ducked, but almost fainted when he saw the plowed furrows cut into the grass next to him - four parallel lines which were the sharp imprints of Lucy's clawed hand. If he had struck a little to the left, Tommy would have lost his head and would have had nowhere to hang his glasses.

He screamed. 'I'm coming!' I yelled, and flew forward. This was too much for me, I knew. I needed help. 'Michael? Michael! Where are you?' I shouted heaven-wards.

Lucy was now moving downfield, after Harold Smyth.

Gerry saw now that the field was in complete chaos. The ball had been booted downfield by Fran. Which meant, considering her now powerless position, that it arced a mere fifteen yards toward the midfield line. Gerry powered toward it, praying that the four separate small brains in his arms and legs would take orders from the control centre between his ears. He toed the ball neatly.

Downfield, he heard someone scream his name. Andy Townsend waved madly. What with all the confusion, the French were completely out of position. Gerry glanced at the clock. Only thirty more seconds left in the match! Awkwardly, he hit the ball. It skittered down the pitch, in Townsend's general direction. The Irish captain had to come forward a little. But the kick would do ...

Big Jimmy, meanwhile, had started to recover from the shock of felling the referee. In fact, he saw the referee walking in circles around the pitch. Around and around and around. The ref didn't seem to know what was going on. Neither did Big Jimmy, for that matter.

Slowly, he stood up. Stood up right in front of an immensely surprised Lucky Lucy who was power

122

diving toward a shrieking Harold Smyth.

'SHMMHHSSSSHH.' Lucky hit Big Jimmy like a bug hitting the side of a steamroller. Big Jimmy only staggered a little. Lucky Lucy looked as if it had been creamed by a fly swatter. It shook its head a little, trying to come to.

As it happened, Lucky Lucy stood in front of the goal. Right in front of it. The vision of the Devil scared the French keeper to death, naturally, and now Lucky Lucy owned the goal. Which meant that he was most pleased when he looked up to see Gerry Larkin stumbling towards him.

'LARKIN,' it whispered in its large voice. 'YOU'RE DEAD!' He stood, then, waiting. The humongous claws stretched out in front of him, ready to carve Gerry Larkin into mincemeat.

I saw that Gerry was in mortal danger and started screaming for Michael again. But it was too late, I thought. Then I saw the ball, and suddenly I knew that everything was going to be all right ...

Andy took the pass from Gerry patiently. All heck had broken out on the field, but that didn't matter. They were in injury time, now, maybe twenty seconds left. He looked around the field. Everyone on the Irish side seemed to be either out of action or running in the opposite direction.

Two French players were descending on him now. He had to make his move. Quick. Then, out of the corner of his eye, Andy saw the running form of Gerry Larkin make its way out of the mists of mortal combat. The captain yelled at him, telling him to keep going, motioning him forward.

Gerry saw the signal. He charged toward the net,

looking for an opening. Then, he saw Lucky Lucy waiting for him, waiting to turn Gerry, the team player that had broken the contract, into chopped liver. Gerry kept running. He no longer had his immense power. He no longer had his hotfoot. But I like to think that he remembered what I had said back in the locker room. Gerry had learned to believe in himself.

It was like a day-dream. The Irish striker ran forward, then stopped suddenly, not wanting to commit himself. The French defensive back moved forward. The striker faked to the right easily, moving deftly back upfield, leaving the Frenchman in his wake.

Readying himself, the Irishman glanced toward the team captain. The incredibly capable midfielder looked right, then left, then hit the ball deftly. Powering up over the helpless heads of the French side, the ball reached its great height, then plummeted toward the waiting Irish rookie, the striker who this day would prove himself ...

... he watched the ball all the way down. He would not let it touch the ground. Not this time. His great leg moved back like a coiled spring, hanging in the balance for a moment, taut with the power that was there. And then releasing! Striking the ball surely, with huge power. The ball was rocketing ... R O C K E T I N G ... through the air, hitting the huge ruddy keeper in the belly. The strike so powerful that the keeper couldn't keep its hands on it, despite its immense strength ... the ball careening through its arms, striking the net with such energy that it hung there for a moment before falling.

And now, he heard them: the crowd of one hundred thousand fans, their voices swelling, sending his name on wings high over the stadium and into the book of football history ...

'LARKIN! LARKIN! LARKIN!'

'Larkin! Larkin! Larkin!' The noise was non-stop. This was no dream! The power of the screaming fans hit him almost physically, hit him until he got pummelled by his exuberant team-mates as they hurtled through the air toward him. 'You did it!' they screamed. 'We won! We won the World Cup!'

Fran was the last to grab him. She hugged him; they were both suddenly embarrassed. 'You did it, didn't you, Larkin?' she screamed.

'We all did it,' Gerry screamed back.

And the seven of them, surrounded by the senior Irish players and a multitude of grateful fans, stood whacking each other on the backs. And when the crowds had dispersed, and the teams were walking into the locker room, a grateful Irish Coach, too stubborn to be kept off the field, watched them move off on the shoulders of grateful fans. He watched a lad named Gerry Larkin and a girl named Fran Clifford and a handful of other young players, and said simply, 'They'll be back. You watch. They'll be back.'

As for Lucky Lucy? Well, I got lucky there, myself. Winded from the might of Gerry Larkin's amazing strike into its solar plexus, Lucy folded up like a sick cow. Michael, having heard my cries for help, finally decided to come down in assistance. It took a while, but we managed to bundle Lucy on home.

He won't be bothering anyone for some time. No, sir! I only wish that we could keep him under lock and key for a few millennia or centuries or even a couple of weeks, but that's just not possible.

And as for Larkin's Lot? Well, let me tell you. They were sure glad to get their souls back. But I don't think they like losing any more. Nope, they don't like losing one little bit. And you know, they don't have to ...

But I'll have to confess one thing to you right now. You might as well know that they didn't exactly win all on their own. You see, I had a word with someone I know. A pretty powerful person. And, well, She sort of gave them a special something that they all needed. A little bit of extra-special energy. Come to think of it, I guess they still have it. But that's another story, isn't it?

For now, rest assured that Gerry, Fran, Harold, Big Jimmy, Tommy Reynolds and the Bright Brothers are still playing football. They win sometimes, and they lose sometimes. But I think they have a great time no matter what happens ... because all they do is try their best.

Oh, and finally ... if you have a special wish, go ahead and send it my way. It will blast into space on a great blue bolt of light, along with the other thousands of wishes. As Problem Wish Assistant First Class, I promise I'll do what I can to help.

Like I say, you'll get what you want only if you believe in yourself ...